"Autumn Pulaski Only Has Her Cockamamy Four-Week Rule Because She Knows It Will Make Guys That Much More Determined To Go Out With Her."

Sean Monahan waited for his pronouncement to sink in.

His brother Finn studied him. "So what makes you think that you could avoid being so bamboozled yourself?"

"Like I said, I know women," Sean reiterated. "I'm hip to her game before we even play it. I will come out the winner. In more ways than one."

"You really think so?" Finn asked.

Sean nodded. "Hey, if there's anybody out there who can last longer than four weeks with Autumn Pulaski," he said with a smile, "I'm the man."

Finn eyed Sean with much consideration. Then, right when it occurred to Sean, at the very back of his brain, that he might have just steered himself toward a deadly cliff, Finn uttered the words that, for thirty-four years, had tolled the death knell for Sean's good sense.

"Prove it, little brother," Finn said knowingly. "Prove it."

Dear Reader,

The year 2000 has been a special time for Silhouette, as we've celebrated our 20th anniversary. Readers from all over the world have written to tell us what they love about our books, and we'd like to share with you part of a letter from Carolyn Dann of Grand Bend, Ontario, who's a fan of Silhouette Desire. Carolyn wrote, "I like the storylines…the characters…the front covers… All the characters in the books are the kind of people you like to read about. They're all down-to-earth, everyday people." And as a grand finale to our anniversary year, Silhouette Desire offers six of your favorite authors for an especially memorable month's worth of passionate, powerful, provocative reading!

We begin the lineup with the always wonderful Barbara Boswell's MAN OF THE MONTH, *Irresistible You,* in which a single woman nine months pregnant meets her perfect hero while on jury duty. The incomparable Cait London continues her exciting miniseries FREEDOM VALLEY with *Slow Fever.* Against a beautiful Montana backdrop, the oldest Bennett sister is courted by a man who spurned her in their teenage years. And *A Season for Love,* in which Sheriff Jericho Rivers regains his lost love, continues the new miniseries MEN OF BELLE TERRE by beloved author BJ James.

Don't miss the thrilling conclusion to the Desire miniseries FORTUNE'S CHILDREN: THE GROOMS in Peggy Moreland's *Groom of Fortune.* Elizabeth Bevarly will delight you with *Monahan's Gamble.* And *Expecting the Boss's Baby* is the launch title of Leanne Banks's new miniseries, MILLION DOLLAR MEN, which offers wealthy, philanthropic bachelors guaranteed to seduce you.

We hope all readers of Silhouette Desire will treasure the gift of this special month.

Happy holidays!

Joan Marlow Golan

Joan Marlow Golan
Senior Editor, Silhouette Desire

Please address questions and book requests to:
Silhouette Reader Service
U.S.: 3010 Walden Ave., P.O. Box 1325, Buffalo, NY 14269
Canadian: P.O. Box 609, Fort Erie, Ont. L2A 5X3

Monahan's Gamble
ELIZABETH BEVARLY

Published by Silhouette Books
America's Publisher of Contemporary Romance

For Eathel and Rex Bellaver,
two of the funnest people I know.

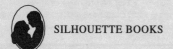 SILHOUETTE BOOKS

ISBN 0-373-76337-9

MONAHAN'S GAMBLE

Copyright © 2000 by Elizabeth Bevarly

This edition published by arrangement with Harlequin Books S.A.

Visit Silhouette at www.eHarlequin.com

Printed in U.S.A.

Books by Elizabeth Bevarly

ELIZABETH BEVARLY

is an honors graduate of the University of Louisville and achieved her dream of writing full-time before she even turned thirty! At heart, she is also an avid voyager who once helped navigate a friend's thirty-five-foot sailboat across the Bermuda Triangle. Her dream is to one day have her own sailboat, a beautifully renovated older model forty-two-footer, and to enjoy the freedom and tranquillity seafaring can bring. Elizabeth likes to think she has a lot in common with the characters she creates, people who know love and life go hand in hand. And she's getting some firsthand experience with motherhood, as well—she and her husband have a six-year-old son, Eli.

Desire

MAN OF THE MONTH

#1333 Irresistible You
Barbara Boswell

Freedom Valley

#1334 Slow Fever
Cait London

MEN of Belle Terre

#1335 A Season for Love
BJ James

Grooms

#1336 Groom of Fortune
Peggy Moreland

#1337 Monahan's Gamble
Elizabeth Bevarly

MILLION DOLLAR MEN

#1338 Expecting the Boss's Baby
Leanne Banks

Romance

Bachelor Gulch

#1486 Sky's Pride and Joy
Sandra Steffen

#1487 Hunter's Vow
Susan Meier

THE BRUBAKER BRIDES

#1488 Montana's Feisty Cowgirl
Carolyn Zane

SINGLE DOCTOR DADS

#1489 Rachel and the M.D.
Donna Clayton

Storks Express

#1490 Mixing Business...with Baby
Diana Whitney

#1491 His Special Delivery
Belinda Barnes

Special Edition

AND BABY MAKES THREE THE NEXT GENERATION

#1363 The Delacourt Scandal
Sherryl Woods

#1364 The McCaffertys: Thorne
Lisa Jackson

#1365 The Cowboy's Gift-Wrapped Bride
Victoria Pade

Rumor Has It... **#1366 Lara's Lover**
Penny Richards

#1367 Mother in a Moment
Allison Leigh

Here Come the Brides **#1368 Expectant Bride-To-Be**
Nikki Benjamin

Intimate Moments

#1045 Special Report
Merline Lovelace/Maggie Price/
Debra Cowan

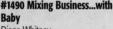
A Year of Loving Dangerously **#1046 Strangers When We Married**
Carla Cassidy

36 HOURS **#1047 A Very...Pregnant New Year's**
Doreen Roberts

#1048 Mad Dog and Annie
Virginia Kantra

#1049 Mirror, Mirror
Linda Randall Wisdom

#1050 Everything But a Husband
Karen Templeton

One

There was nothing Sean Monahan enjoyed more than a game of cutthroat poker—unless it was a game of cutthroat poker played with a couple of his brothers. Sean was a gambler by nature, and a winner by birth. When he took chances, they invariably played out. And there wasn't much that gave him a bigger charge than fleecing his own flesh and blood.

Hey, that was just the kind of guy he was.

He and two of his brothers and two of their friends had only been playing poker for an hour, and already Sean's take was substantial. Best of all, he'd won most of his loot from his big brother, Finn. At this rate he'd have the down payment for that new roadster he'd been lusting after for months, in no time at all.

As he sat in the kitchen of Finn's expansive—and, Sean knew, *expensive*—condo, he gazed over a pretty decent hand at Cullen, one of his three younger brothers, and tried to gauge his sibling's hand by the expression on Cullen's face. As he did so, Sean puffed diligently on a very nice cigar, inhaled the spicy aroma of Finn's famous five-alarm chili and pondered whether or not he should get up for another beer or simply wait until someone else did—preferably Finn—and have him get Sean one, too.

Life just didn't get any better than this.

"Where's Will tonight?" he asked, having noted the glaring absence of Will Darrow, Finn's best friend since childhood and a staple at the group's twice-monthly poker/chili/beerfest.

His big brother chuckled low in a way that Sean found very interesting. "Will's got some things to work out," Finn said cryptically. "Issues. The boy's got a lot on his mind these days."

Charlie Hofstetter, another member of the all-male poker quintet, glanced up from his own hand. "Is that why he's been so cranky for the past week? What's up with that? Will's never cranky."

Finn's cryptic chuckles eased into a mysterious grin. He puffed once on his own cigar and dragged a hand through his black hair. "Like I said. Issues."

"But what does that mean?" Sean insisted, shoving back a fistful of his own dark locks, thinking he and Finn both needed a cut.

"You'll all find out soon enough," Finn told him. But he said nothing more to elaborate.

Sean muttered an impatient sound. "You always think you know everything, Finn."

"That's 'cause I do know everything," his big brother stated with all certainty.

Sean wanted very badly to argue with that statement, but he knew better. Somehow Finn always did seem to know everything. It was a damned annoying trait for an older brother to have.

"Gordon's missing tonight, too. Where's he?" Sean asked further, wondering why none of the other four men had offered an explanation for it already.

Cullen sighed dramatically. "Gordon's nursing a broken heart," he said in a girlie, wistful voice as he puffed on his cigar.

Sean chuckled. "That's some feat. I didn't realize Gordon had a heart to break. Who's the lucky girl?"

Cullen shifted his cigar from one side of his mouth to the other. "Autumn Pulaski," he mumbled around the obstruction.

"Autumn Pulaski?" Ted Embry, the fifth member of the group cried incredulously. "What was he doing going out with her in the first place? Everybody knows Autumn never dates anyone for longer than a month."

"A lunar month, at that," Charlie pointed out.

"She is such an oddball," Ted remarked.

"Free spirit," Finn corrected him. "I believe the correct label for a woman like her is 'free spirit.'"

"'One hot tomata' seems like a more appropriate label for her to me," Cullen added.

None of the other men disagreed with the evaluation, including Sean. In fact, he noted, all of the other men observed a moment of worshipful silence in honor of the occasion. So what could Sean do but respect that by observing a moment of reverential meditation himself.

Then Ted broke the spell. "Okay, so I guess I can see why Gordon was going out with her. But he should have realized there'd be a time limit on the thing. He shouldn't have involved his heart. Hell, he never should've involved any other body part than his—"

"Oh, man, did you see her at Josh and Louisa's wedding last month?" Charlie—delicately—interrupted.

Oh, man, indeed, Sean echoed to himself. Had he ever seen her. She'd looked good enough to— Well. A number of ideas erupted in his brain at the recollection, all of them vivid, none of them decent. She'd worn a paper-thin dress of some flowery, gauzy fabric, and every time she'd crossed in front of the reception hall windows that bright, sunny afternoon, every male breath in the place had gone still.

She might as well have been wearing nothing at all, so clearly outlined had her body been under that dress. It had more than made up for the wide, ridiculous-looking straw hat she'd worn on her head, the one whose brim had been big enough to obscure the beautiful face beneath. Then again, Sean thought, few people had been looking at Autumn's face that day.

Normally, though, that wasn't the case at all. Because in addition to being a 'free spirit,' as Finn had tagged her, she was also, most definitely, what Cullen had called her, too. One. Hot. Tomata. True to her name, Autumn's hair was a tumble of auburn curls that spilled in a rich, riotous cascade down to the middle of her back. Her eyes were the color and clarity of good Irish whisky—and every bit as intoxicating. Finely sculpted cheekbones and one of those faintly turned-up noses gave the impression that she had posed for any number of classical paintings. And her mouth...

Oh, her *mouth*.

Sean could write rhapsodies about that full, luscious, decadent mouth. Her complexion seemed to be perpetually golden, regardless of the season, and somehow Sean knew—he just *knew*—that there were none of those irritating bathing suit lines to mar the color. Autumn Pulaski, free spirit, oddball and one hot tomata, just seemed like the type who would go for nude sunbathing.

"Gordon will get over it," Charlie said confidently as he went back to arranging his hand. "Every man Autumn's ever dated has gotten over it. Eventually."

"I still don't see why Gordon got involved in the first place," Ted said. "I mean, he's actually been looking for a long-term relationship, and everybody in town knows that Autumn's hard-and-fast rule has always been that no man—*no man*—will ever last longer than four weeks when it comes to dating her.''

"Why does she have that rule, anyway?" Cullen asked. "I never could understand the reasoning behind it."

Sean glanced up just in time to see Ted shrug. "No idea," Ted said. "But ever since she moved to Marigold— what?…two years ago?—she's always made that clear. I get the feeling it's a rule she's had in place for a lo-o-o-ong time. I'll open," he added carelessly, tossing two chips into the middle of the table. Just as carelessly he continued, "Hey, Gordon was lucky. At least he got in the full four weeks with her before she dumped him. A lot of guys never even make it to the half-moon.

"She is such an oddball," Ted said again.

"Free spirit," Finn corrected once more.

"Well, whatever she is, I'm not asking her out," Cullen announced. "I have enough trouble with women, thank you very much. I don't need one starting a timer on me the minute she opens the door."

"You and me both," Charlie agreed. "I don't think there's a man in Marigold—hell, in the entire state of Indiana—who could last longer than four weeks with Autumn Pulaski."

Sean shook his head slowly and tossed two chips into the pot to see Ted's opening bid. "I could date Autumn Pulaski for more than four weeks," he stated quite seriously—and not a little proudly.

"You?" a chorus of incredulous echoes erupted from around the table.

Sean gaped his indignation at the disbelief that was so evident in each of his compatriots. "Yeah, me. What's so unbelievable about that?"

Each of the men gazed at him in silence for a moment,

as if they couldn't imagine why he would even ask such a thing. But it was Finn who challenged, ''What makes you think Autumn would go out with you for *any* length of time, let alone more than her very standard, very adamant, lunar month?''

Sean shrugged. ''I've got a way about me.''

Now each of his compatriots laughed. Quite raucously, in fact, something Sean decided he probably shouldn't dwell on.

But he did. ''Well, what the hell is so funny?'' he demanded.

''You've got a way about you all right, boyo,'' Finn said through his chuckles. ''But it's not necessarily the one you think.''

''Hey!'' Sean cried even more indignantly. ''Women *love* me.''

''Autumn's different,'' Cullen said.

Sean took some heart in the fact that at least Cullen didn't deny that women loved him. After all, there was so much evidence to the contrary. Women really did love Sean. Often for weeks on end.

Sean threw his little brother an indulgent look. ''Autumn's not different,'' he said. ''Women are all alike. Deep down they all want one thing.''

Four male faces gazed back at him, this time in very expectant silence. But it was Finn who said—and he was clearly battling a giggle when he did so—''Oh?''

Sean nodded.

His big brother grinned tolerantly. ''And what, oh omniscient knower of women, would that one thing be that they all want?''

''Equal pay for equal work,'' Cullen offered with a smile before Sean had a chance to answer.

''No, men who do their own laundry,'' Ted piped up with a chuckle.

"No, men who not only do their own laundry but sort by light and dark, too," Charlie threw in for good measure.

"Oh, hardy-har-har-har," Sean replied. "Very funny, wise guys."

Eventually the men stopped laughing—again. And when they did, Finn turned a more serious—sort of—gaze on his brother. "Truly, Sean," he said. "What is this one thing that all women want? We're on the edge of our seats."

Sean lifted his chin a bit defensively. "A wedding ring," he said.

Cullen narrowed his eyes at his brother. "Gee, they can get one of those down at Huck's Pawnshop for twenty bucks. Thirty if they want one that's not hot."

"A wedding ring with a husband attached," Sean clarified—not that any clarification would be necessary if it weren't for the fact that he was sitting at a table with his four moronic friends and relatives.

"Oh, hey, I'm sorry, but Huck doesn't include that kind of service with his pawn," Cullen said. "A man has to draw the line somewhere."

Sean sighed impatiently. "You know what I mean," he said evenly. "Women—all women—want to get married. They want to find that one special someone and settle down forever, then milk the poor sap for everything he's got— socially, financially, emotionally, spiritually, you name it. Women want to be wives. That's all there is to it."

There wasn't a single comment from anyone present at the table for a moment, then, "Stand back, everybody," Finn said mildly, "I think his brain is about to blow."

Sean growled under his breath. "Look, all I'm saying is that if Autumn Pulaski has this ridiculous rule about not dating anybody for more than a month—"

"A lunar month," Cullen reminded him.

"A lunar month," Sean said through gritted teeth, "then she's only doing it to rouse more interest."

Finn eyed him levelly. "You know, Sean, I think I speak for everyone here when I say, 'Huh?'"

The other three men nodded their agreement.

Sean rolled his eyes. "Autumn wants to make herself seem more appealing, in order to snag a man," he said. "She thinks that if she has this no-dating-after-a-month—"

"A lunar month," Cullen corrected him again.

"—rule," Sean continued, ignoring his younger brother, "then it'll just make guys that much more determined to date her for more than a *lunar*," he said before Cullen could interrupt him, "month."

"So you don't think she's serious when she says she'll never date a man for longer than four weeks?" Ted asked.

"Of course she's not serious," Sean said with much conviction.

Ted eyed him curiously. "Then...why hasn't she ever dated any man in Marigold for more than four weeks?"

Sean shrugged. "She hasn't met the right guy, that's all," he said. "That's another reason she's got this alleged rule. So she can let the less-desirable guys go without a messy confrontation."

"And you think you're the right guy," Charlie assumed.

"I'm certainly a damn sight better than any of you mooks," he said smugly. "*And* Gordon."

"Yes, well, you always were a legend in your own mind," Finn remarked mildly.

"I'm serious," Sean insisted. "Autumn Pulaski only has her cockamamie lunar-month rule because she knows it will just make guys that much more determined to go out with her. Then, when she finally reels in the one she wants, she'll have the guy so bamboozled, she'll be able to wrap him up in silver wedding paper with a big, white bow."

Cullen studied him with much speculation. "So what makes you think that you could, in addition to dating her for more than four weeks, avoid being so bamboozled and wrapped up like a wedding gift yourself?''

''Like I said, I know women,'' Sean reiterated matter-of-factly. ''I'm hip to her game before we even start to play it. *I* will come out the winner. In more ways than one.''

''You really think so?'' Finn asked.

Sean nodded. ''Hey, if there's anybody out there who can last longer than a lunar month with Autumn Pulaski,'' he said with a smile, ''I'm the man.''

Finn chewed his lower lip thoughtfully for a moment, eyeing Sean with much consideration. Then, right when it occurred to Sean, at the very back of his brain, that he might have just steered himself toward a deadly cliff—but much too late for him to backpedal out of the fatal fall— Finn uttered the words that, for thirty-four years, had tolled the death knell for Sean's good sense:

''Prove it, little brother,'' Finn said knowingly. ''Prove it.''

Autumn Pulaski was wrestling with a large mass of dough, one that would eventually be a nice loaf of seven-grain onion dill, when she heard the tinkle of the bell over the front door in the shop area of the Autumn's Harvest Bakery. Normally that door would still be locked this early in the morning, but she'd brought some things in through the front earlier and had neglected to lock up behind her-self. It had hardly seemed necessary, because few people in Marigold, Indiana, were even awake this time of morn-ing—particularly on a Saturday. And those who *were* awake were almost certainly not out and about. And those who *were* out and about were either working themselves, or were on their way to go fishing.

''We're not open yet!'' she called out toward the shop. ''Come back at seven!''

But instead of hearing the tinkle of the bell as her 6 a.m.

customer left, Autumn heard silence instead, indicating the visitor was still out in the shop. She was more curious about that development than she was concerned for her safety. This was, after all, Marigold, Indiana. In other words, Small Town, U.S.A. The only crimes that occurred here were crimes of fashion.

Plus, she wasn't alone in the bakery. She was working with two of the teenage girls she'd hired for the summer, not to mention Louis, who always came in to help her in the mornings. And Louis was six foot seven, had shoulders the size of the Hoover Dam and forearms as big as a Bekins truck. His long, gray beard was braided down to nearly his very ample waist, and a tattoo on his right bicep read, quite simply, Raise Hell. Nobody, but nobody messed with Louis.

And nobody made better cream puffs, either.

Autumn sighed heavily and jerked her head to the side, pitching her long, fat, auburn braid over one shoulder. She wiped her hands on her white apron, tugged the sleeves of her white peasant blouse down over her elbows, and did her best to straighten the white kerchief she had tied around her head, pirate-style. And she abandoned, for now, the heap of seven-grain onion dill that taunted her, and went out to the shop to assess the situation.

Immediately she wished she had stayed in the kitchen and sent Louis instead. Not because of any threat to her personal safety—well, not any criminal threat at any rate. But because Sean Monahan stood front and center in the middle of her shop, looking adorably sleep rumpled and half dozing, his slumberous blue eyes even sexier than usual. And all Autumn could think was, *Oh, no.*

Of course, she thought further, finding one of the Monahan brothers in her immediate sphere of existence was bound to have happened sooner or later. This was, after all, Marigold, Indiana, where everybody knew everybody, and everybody met everybody just about every day. She only wished this episode could have happened a lot later than it had.

Then again, she thought further still, she supposed she should be grateful this encounter had taken two years to occur, even if she had made every effort to ensure that such a meeting *never took place. Because the last thing Autumn wanted or needed was to have a handsome, charming, eligible man in her immediate sphere of existence. Her entire move from Chicago to Marigold had been driven by just that need. Or, rather, that lack of need. Or something like that.*

*Two times—two times—*Autumn had found herself involved in relationships with handsome, charming, eligible men, men who had promised to love her and honor her and cherish her, in sickness and in health, till death did them part. Unfortunately, the men in question had just never made those promises at the altar. They'd *said* they would make those promises at the altar, but neither of them— *neither of them—*had shown up at the respective altars where they had been scheduled to appear.

Fool her once, shame on them, Autumn reasoned. Fool her twice, shame on her. Fool her three times, and it was going to be necessary for her to enter a convent. Which would pose problems on a variety of levels, not the least of which was the fact that Autumn wasn't Catholic. She was an Emersonian Transcendentalist. So the nun thing wasn't really going to be doable. Therefore, she was just going to have to make sure there wasn't a third time. She'd entertained a lot of possibilities about how to ensure that, and had decided on the one plan that had sounded best— moving to a small town where there were no handsome, charming, eligible men to sidetrack her, and doing what she'd always dreamed about doing: opening her own bread bakery.

So that was why Autumn had fled to Marigold—to follow a dream, and to get away from men like Sean Monahan. She had reasoned that small-town life would be a hugely welcome change from the big-city lifestyle she had embraced for so long. She had also thought that a small town like Marigold would be infinitely safer than big-city living. Not because of the crime factor—though, granted, Marigold's nonexistent crime rate was a nice by-product of her change of venue. But more because small towns were supposed to be utterly bereft of handsome, charming eligible men—unlike Chicago, which had seemed to be overflowing with them.

Autumn needed a respite—a nice, *lo-o-o-ong* respite, like maybe for the rest of her life—from handsome, charming, eligible men. Marigold, Indiana, had seemed like the kind of place that would have almost none. Small towns were supposed to drive young singles away in, well, droves. Instead, no sooner had she unpacked her belongings and opened her bakery than she had wandered out into the town itself to make friends…only to discover that Marigold, Indiana, was overflowing with handsome, charming, eligible men, from the head of the Chamber of Commerce—who, thankfully, was happily married—right down to the local mechanic—who, wouldn't you know it, was not.

And right at the top of that pile were the Monahan brothers—all five of them. *Five* of them, she marveled now as she gazed anxiously at Sean. As if *one* wouldn't have been overwhelming enough for the universe—or, at the very least, for Autumn Pulaski. Each one of them had piercing blue eyes and dark, silky hair and finely chiseled features. Each one was a piece of Greek-god artwork just waiting to be worshipped. Each one was handsome. Each one was charming. Each one was eligible.

Damn. Just her luck.

"Hello," she said to Sean now, trying not to notice his

piercing blue eyes or his dark, silky hair or his finely chiseled features.

But doing that left her nothing to focus on except for his Greek-god-artwork physique, and that was no help at all. Clad in lovingly faded, form-fitting Levi's and an equally faded and form-fitting black T-shirt, his entire body fairly rippled with muscle and sinew and, oh, my stars, it was just too much for Autumn this early in the day, before she'd even had her second cup of coffee. Looking at Sean Monahan was making her feel sluggish and indolent and warm, and very much in the mood to return to her bed. Except…not alone. And…not for sleeping.

"Can I help you?" she asked, hoping her voice didn't sound as sluggish and indolent and warm as it—and the rest of her—felt.

Belatedly she realized she probably shouldn't have asked the question at all. Not only did it offer him an opportunity to say something flirtatious—and everyone in Marigold knew that flirtatious was Sean Monahan's natural state—but there was nothing for her to help him with. The store wasn't open yet. There was no bread to sell. Then again, knowing what she did of Sean Monahan, which was surprisingly a lot, considering the fact that she'd never met him formally—or even casually—he probably wasn't interested in her bread, anyway.

But before she could make clear the fact that she had nothing to offer him—nothing of the bread persuasion, at any rate—Sean smiled at her, and her entire body went *zing*. Truly. *Zing*. She'd had no idea that the human body could, in fact, go *zing*, until now. But that was exactly what Sean's smile did to her. Because it was the kind of smile a man really shouldn't smile at a woman unless they were extremely well—nay, *intimately*—acquainted.

"I just wanted to get a big, strapping cup of coffee," he

said, cranking up the wattage on his smile to a near-blinding setting.

Oh, Autumn really wished he hadn't said the words *big* and *strapping,* because, inevitably, they drove her thoughts—and her gaze, dammit—right back to that Greek-god-artwork body of his.

"My coffeemaker went belly-up on me this morning," he continued.

Oh, she really wished he hadn't said the word *belly.*

"And I have to make a long drive today—"

Oh, she really wished he hadn't said the word *long.*

"—and no place else is open this early."

Oh, she really wished he hadn't said the word *open.*

Stop it, Autumn, she berated herself. Not one word the man had uttered had been in any way suggestive, but as he'd spoken, somehow Sean Monahan made her feel as if he'd just dragged a slow, sensuous finger along the inside of her thigh. How did he do it?

"We, uh…" Autumn began eloquently. She swallowed with some difficulty, and tried not to notice just how incredibly handsome, charming and eligible he was. "We, ah…we're not ope— Um, I mean…we're, ah…we're closed, too," she managed to say—eventually—still struggling over the word *open,* because that was exactly what she wanted to do at the moment. Open herself. To Sean Monahan. Mentally, emotionally, spiritually, physically, sexually. That was always her immediate response to handsome, charming, eligible men. Which was why it was so important that she avoid them at all costs.

He met her gaze levelly as he jacked up the power on his smile a bit more—Autumn had to bite back a wince at just how dazzling he was—then jutted a thumb over his shoulder, toward the front door. She squeezed her eyes shut tight, trying not to notice how the muscles in his abdomen fairly danced as he completed the gesture.

"Your front door's open," he pointed out.

It certainly is, Autumn thought before she could stop herself. *And why don't you just come on right inside?*

Immediately she snapped her eyes open and pushed the thought away. This was, without question, the very last thing she needed, today or any day. She swallowed with some difficulty, her mouth going dry when the chorus line that was his torso synchronized as he dropped his hand back to his side.

"Yes, well, the door may be open, but the shop isn't," she told him, proud of herself for not stumbling once over the proclamation.

"I smell coffee brewing," he said.

"That's not for sale, it's for the workers," she replied. "We're a bakery, Mr. Monahan, not a beanery."

His blue eyes, so clear and limitless, reflected laughter and good humor, and something else upon which she told herself she absolutely should not speculate. "You know my name," he said softly.

Oops. "Well, I know you're a Monahan. It is a small town. And you Monahan boys all look alike," she lied. "I just don't know which Monahan boy you are."

Oh, my. Two falsehoods before dawn. Autumn was definitely going to create some bad karma with that. And why on earth was she referring to him as a "boy"? Sean Monahan was quite undeniably a man, and probably five or six years her senior, to boot.

He took a few steps forward, his shoes scuffing softly over the terra-cotta tiles as he came, his mouth quirked into that sleepy, sexy smile—the one that made him look as if he'd just made sweet, sensational love to its recipient, successfully and repeatedly. He only stopped moving because the counter hindered his progress, but he still leaned forward and folded his arms over the glass top, right in front of where Autumn was standing. He was so close she could see the dark shadow of his freshly shaved beard, could smell the clean, soapy scent of him, could fairly feel the warmth of his body creeping over the counter to mingle with her own.

Instinct told her to take a giant step backward…and then run like the wind as far as she could. Instead she stood firm, waiting to see what he would do next. And as was always the case when it came to handsome, charming, eligible men, that was Autumn's fatal mistake.

Because Sean Monahan's piercing blue eyes pierced her right down to her soul, warming a place inside her she had forgotten could feel warmth. And then, "I really was hoping for a cup of coffee," he said softly. "But you know, Autumn, now that you mention it, there *is* something else you can do for me, too."

Two

Surprisingly, Sean had never actually stood this close to Autumn Pulaski before now, and he couldn't help but wonder why not. Normally he gravitated toward attractive, single women faster than the planets spun through space, yet this one had somehow eluded him until he'd made this very assertive, very specific, foray into her life. It was especially odd considering the fact that she'd lived in Marigold for more than two years now—he could vaguely recall the grand opening of her bakery three springtimes ago. And his apartment was, quite literally, just around the corner, something else that made astonishing the fact that he had never before been in such close quarters with the elusive Ms. Pulaski. Either his timing had really suffered over the last couple of years—which was laughably unlikely—or Ms. Pulaski went out of her way to make sure their paths had never crossed.

In a word, *Hmm.*

At any rate, Sean had never realized until now just how strikingly beautiful she really was. And he hadn't realized she smelled so good, either, like apple tarts and cinnamon buns, and something strangely exotic and spicy that blended perfectly with the homey aroma of freshly baked bread. It threw him for a momentary loop, and for the first time in his life he had no idea what to say.

Which was odd, because when he'd entered the bakery only moments ago, he'd known exactly what he wanted to say. In fact, he'd practiced his speech last night until the words had flowed fluidly and confidently and not a little seductively, if he did say so himself, even though he had pretty much decided to avoid the seduction thing—for now. At the moment, though, for the life of him Sean could remember none of what he had rehearsed. All he could do was gaze into Autumn's whisky-gold eyes, inhale deeply her cinnamon scent, absorb the way her peasant blouse dipped pleasantly above the swells of her very generous breasts and battle the urge to go much, much faster in his seduction than he had initially planned.

Wait a minute. Back up. Think again, Monahan.

It wasn't seduction he was planning, he reminded himself again. Not necessarily, at any rate. Not specifically. Not yet. He just wanted to last more than four weeks with the enigmatic Ms. Pulaski, right? In fact, he had to make it through not one, but *two,* lunar months, if Sean was going to win the dare that Finn had challenged him to complete last weekend.

He was still ticked off at himself for having set himself up for, not to mention having succumbed so easily to, that dare. He should have known better than to boast about anything in front of Finn, even something at which he was more than confident he could succeed. Finn jumped on a dare faster than you could say "Prove it, little brother," especially when Sean was on the receiving end of it. They'd competed in such a way since they were boys. And invariably, dammit, Finn always came out the victor.

Well, not this time, Sean promised himself. If Finn had challenged him to make it through two lunar months with Autumn Pulaski, then by God, Sean would do it. Of course, that did give him ample time for seduction, he told himself, should such a thing come up—to put it crassly. Then again, he didn't necessarily want to seduce Autumn, did he? Then again, he *was* Sean Monahan, the downfall of many a woman both here and abroad. Well, maybe not abroad. But as far away as Bloomington, which was more than a lot of guys in Marigold could say. So if seduction just sort of happened, that would be okay. Sean wouldn't go looking for it, but he would certainly leave himself open to the possibility.

His current avenue of thoughts, although certainly pleasant, gave Sean no fuel whatsoever in the What-do-I-say-next? department, so he did what he always did whenever he was at a loss for words—which, granted, hadn't really happened before. But doing what he did next seemed a logical reaction. He smiled his most seductive, suggestive smile and cocked a dark brow in just such a way as to make women the world over—or at least as far away as Bloomington—swoon with delight. Autumn Pulaski, however, he noted right away, was very good at hiding her feelings. Because, amazingly enough, not only did she *not* swoon with delight, she didn't even seem to notice the change in his expression.

Damn, she was good.

"And what is it I might do for you, Mr. Monahan?" she asked in as businesslike a voice as Sean had ever heard, jarring him back to the matter at hand.

"Well, first off," he said, "you can *stop* addressing me as Mr. Monahan and *start* calling me Sean."

She offered no outward indication that she had even

heard him, but inquired again, "And what is it I might do for you, Mr. Monahan?"

He blew out a faintly impatient breath, cocked his eyebrow yet again and tried that seductive-suggestive-smile thing one more time. "Well, for one thing," he began smoothly, "I noticed there's a new moon next week."

She didn't seem to think that significant at all, though, because she only continued to stare at him with a vaguely curious expression. When he said nothing further, she replied, with just the slightest hint of impatience, "I believe you're right. There is indeed a new moon next week. On Wednesday, if memory serves."

He nodded slowly. "As a matter of fact, it *is* on Wednesday. And I think that's very…interesting. Don't you?"

She sighed heavily, as if resigned to some great task. "I suppose one might find it interesting," she agreed, "were one studying astronomy or astrology or astrophysics or Zoroastrianism or one of those other astro-sciences."

"Actually," Sean said, "I don't think Zoroastrianism is an astro-science, per se, but rather a philosophical outlook that's really quite fascina—"

"In any case," she interjected smoothly, folding her elbow on the counter. She cupped her chin in one hand and studied Sean with some intent. "I was under the impression, Mr. Monahan, that you designed computer software for a living. Some of those fantasy-driven games with monsters and caves and large-breasted women, the kind that might be created by someone who was reluctant to leave his childhood behind."

Oh, now *this* was getting interesting, Sean thought. He folded his arm to cup his chin in his hand, mimicking her posture…and bringing their faces within inches of each other. The mingling scents of cinnamon and apples and bread that surrounded her suddenly enveloped him, too, very nearly overwhelming him. And much to Sean's surprise, he realized he wanted nothing more in life than to lean forward a bit more so that he could…nibble her. He was suddenly anxious to know if she tasted as sweet as she smelled.

He bit back a sigh of his own, one that, had he released it, would have no doubt been filled with *much* satisfaction. "I thought you said you didn't know which Monahan I was," he murmured in as smooth a voice as he could manage. "But it sounds like you know me pretty well. Autumn."

She gazed back at him in silence for a moment, with an expression he could only define as…inscrutable. Then, very suddenly, very quickly, "It was a cup of coffee you said you wanted, wasn't it, Mr. Monahan?" she piped up brightly.

Before he had a chance to respond—not that she seemed to want him to respond—she straightened and spun around on her heel. She marched straight through a door Sean deduced must lead to the kitchen, her russet-colored, waist-length braid swaying rhythmically—and not a little seductively, he thought—above luscious-looking hips. Within seconds she returned with a cardboard cup—a really *big* cardboard cup, like the kind for which no sane person would *ever* ask a refill—and thrust it toward him. Fortunately, there was a lid on the cup, so none of it sloshed out to make a mess on the counter…or burn off a layer of her skin. Unfortunately, however, at least for Autumn, that wasn't the main thing Sean had come in to ask for.

"What are you doing Wednesday night?" he asked, ignoring the cup she extended toward him.

Her expression went from inscrutable to…well, quite scrutable…in a nanosecond. Mostly, Sean thought, she looked really confused and not a little panicky. "I—I'm working," she said, thrusting the cup toward him again, more insistently this time.

And again Sean ignored it. "How late?" he asked.

She gaped faintly for a moment, gazing at him as if he had just asked her to come with him to the Casbah, where they could make beautiful music together. Then she shook her head quickly, once, as if to clear it of a muzzying fog…and extended the cup of coffee forward, *very* insistently, *again.* But her conviction seemed to be wavering some as she told him, "I, um, till nine."

He nodded his approval…and continued to ignore the cup of coffee. "Nine," he repeated with interest. "Right about when the sun will be almost down and the new moon will be visible."

She eyed him now with something akin to intrigue and absently licked her lips. Sean considered the simple gesture to be highly erotic. "Actually, Mr. Monahan, new moons aren't visible," she said. "Hence the term 'new.'"

Yeah, yeah, yeah, Sean thought. *Whatever.* "A minor technicality," he assured her aloud. "It'll be a nice night for…" He paused meaningfully. At least, he hoped she considered it a meaningful pause. God knew he sure intended for it to be meaningful. "A lot of things," he finally concluded, likewise meaningfully. "How about we make a night of it, just the two of us?"

Autumn gazed back at Sean Monahan in frank disbelief, trying to tamp down the heat that swirled unhampered in her midsection, trying to assure herself he was *not* doing what he seemed to be doing. He was *not* coming on to her. He was *not* asking her out. He was *not* trying to tell her, with all his discussion of the new moon, that he wanted to be the next man in line to…to…to…

To *date* her.

Was he?

Oh, surely not. Not Sean Monahan. He, of all men in Marigold, was to be steadfastly avoided. That was why she had so steadfastly avoided him ever since coming to town.

Of all the Monahans—and certainly all of them were to be steadfastly avoided—Sean posed the greatest threat. Because although each of the Monahan brothers was handsome and charming and eligible, Sean Monahan was the *most* handsome, the *most* charming and, indeed, the *most* eligible. Where one or two of his brothers did show potential for being the marrying kind—it was widely known that Finn, for example, carried a massive torch for one Violet Demarest, whom Autumn had never met, because Violet no longer lived in Marigold, even if her rather bad reputation did—Sean had never made any secret of his confirmed bachelorhood. On the contrary, Sean seemed to go out of his way to drive home his very absolute intention of remaining single for the rest of his life.

Which, now that Autumn thought a bit more about it, might actually be just the thing she needed in a…date. Someone who wouldn't have expectations of anything lasting. Someone with whom she could just have a casual, easy, fun time of it for a few—or four—weeks. Someone who wouldn't drop to his knees at the end of that four weeks and beg for just one more lunar month, please, for God's sake, just one. Someone who didn't crave permanence, so would never propose marriage and, consequently, would never leave her waiting at the altar, filled with humiliation and horror and self-doubt for the third time in a row.

No, no, no, no, no, a little voice piped up inside her. It wasn't just Sean whom Autumn had to worry about. She had to think about herself, too. Because as troubling as it was to have men falling for her—even though she knew whatever those men felt was only temporary and would soon go away—there was always that chance that Autumn might fall for one of them. Just because that hadn't happened since she'd come to Marigold didn't mean there wouldn't be a first time. Yes, her lunar-month deadline did pretty much prevent any potentially long-lasting feelings. But she did believe that love could happen much more quickly than that. It wasn't likely, of course, but it was possible.

Not that she thought Sean would fall in love with her, because, clearly, he wasn't capable of such a deep, abiding emotion. Otherwise the man would have been married a long time ago, because there was no shortage of women in town who would like to have reeled him in. Women did talk, after all, especially when they were waiting in line to buy something. Something like, oh, say…bread, for instance. Over the past two years, Autumn had heard more than her fair share of gossip about the local citizenry. And Marigold's gossip was unusual in that A, it was seldom malicious and B, it was seldom inaccurate.

Yes, Autumn knew a lot about Sean Monahan. She knew a lot about all of the Monahans, in fact. For instance, she knew that Sean's little sister, Tess, who taught first grade over at Our Lady of Lourdes Catholic School, was, at this very moment, pregnant by a man who'd been forced to go into the Witness Protection Program. Such talk had been rampant in the bakery over the last month or so. And in addition to Finn Monahan's torch bearing on behalf of Violet Demarest, Autumn also knew that Miriam Thornbury, the local librarian, had a major thing for Rory Monahan, even though Rory didn't know she existed. But then, Rory didn't really know anyone existed outside of history books, so that wasn't exactly surprising.

So Autumn had learned much over the past two years through the snippets of information she'd picked up at work. And the one thing that was most evident, above all else, was the fact that Sean Monahan was Marigold's confirmed bachelor, a man who would still be single and womanizing upon his centennial.

Which would make him the perfect candidate for dating,

provided Autumn could be assured that she would be embracing the same kind of lifestyle herself at that age. But she'd learned a long time ago that she wasn't the kind of person who thrived on solitude and independence. No, what she craved was a partnership of the most traditional kind, and a dependence on someone who depended on her in return. She wanted a loving, lasting union with another human being, because she just didn't like being alone. She wanted a wedding. She wanted a husband. She knew that wasn't exactly fashionable for women her age, but there it was all the same. She was naturally gregarious and socially outgoing. She didn't want to spend the rest of her life alone.

Unfortunately, alone was exactly how she *would* be spending her life. Because as much as Autumn wished she could find the perfect partner, she simply could not trust her instincts when it came to judging men. Twice, now, she had been certain she'd found Mr. Right. Twice she had put her lifelong trust in a man she had been sure would love her forever. Twice she had been fully prepared to promise herself to a man for better or for worse, in sickness and in health, till death did them part. And twice she had been egregiously mistaken.

It was so unfair, she thought. The fact that she wanted to be married had caused her to get much too involved with men she shouldn't have, so she couldn't get too involved with men, which meant she would never marry. As much as Autumn yearned for a permanent relationship with someone of the opposite sex, on each of the occasions that she'd attempted one, everything had blown up in her face. She didn't want to suffer the pain of humiliation and loss again. So she suffered the pain of solitude and loneliness instead.

In the past she'd thought about advertising for a roommate, nurturing a friendship with another woman who had the same likes and dislikes she had herself. But deep down, Autumn knew that wasn't the kind of company she really wanted or needed. What she wanted, what she needed, was romance. Not the temporary kind. The permanent kind. The kind that started off breathless and lawless and tumultuous and concluded with two arthritic hands and bifocaled gazes locked in easy, comfortable companionship.

Unfortunately, life experience had taught her that there simply was no such thing. Oh, certainly some people did still find that kind of love, but, clearly, she was not destined for it herself. Two times she had thought she'd found it. Two times she had made the leap. Two times she had enjoyed the breathless and lawless and tumultuous, only to watch it fade to nothing at all. She wasn't likely to make the leap again. Certainly not with a man like Sean Monahan, who was so clearly determined *not* to make a commitment.

"I'm sorry, but I'm busy Wednesday night after work," she said, injecting more conviction into her voice than she felt in her heart.

Sean Monahan's smile fell some, and the light in his eyes dimmed. "Busy?" he echoed, as if he was unfamiliar with the word. Then, to further the image, he added, "I don't understand."

Autumn nibbled her lip thoughtfully and wondered how to verbalize all the troubling, unstructured thoughts that had been tumbling through her brain since she'd found Sean Monahan standing in her shop. Then she noticed how very focused he was on the fact that she was nibbling her lip in thought, so she stopped. When she did, his gaze lifted from her mouth to her eyes, and the look he gave her could have made a glacier spontaneously combust.

Oh. Dear.

"Mr. Monahan—"

"I should go."

They started speaking at the same time and ended at the same time, and something about that—both that and the incandescent sizzle in the air that seemed to arc between them then—made Autumn feel as if their destinies, which until today had never crossed, had suddenly gotten tangled up in a way that would be very difficult to unravel.

"What do I owe you for the coffee?" he asked, reaching deep into his pocket to retrieve some change.

She held up both hands, palm out, as if in surrender, though what she might possibly be surrendering to, she dared not consider. "It's on the house," she told him. "I haven't opened the cash registers yet, so... Consider it a promotional giveaway."

He nodded quickly and muttered his thanks but offered no indication that he intended to leave. Instead he only continued to stare at Autumn's face or, more specifically, her mouth, as if he had some serious plans for it in the not-too-distant future. Then, as if he suddenly realized where his gaze was lingering, he snatched it away, dipping his head to focus instead on the coffee cup that sat on the counter. Very gingerly he reached forward and claimed it, never once so much as glancing at Autumn as he did.

"I gotta go," he said hastily. And without further ado, he made good on the announcement.

For long moments after he left, Autumn stood alone in the shop part of her bakery, gazing out the door he had exited, watching the impending sunrise change the color of the sky above the buildings across the way from heavy black to midnight blue. For some reason she felt breathless and lawless and tumultuous and, at the same time, easy and comfortable and companionable. And there was one other thing she felt, too, she realized. When she remembered the heat in Sean Monahan's gaze and the brightness in his smile, when she recalled how handsome, how charming, how eligible he was...

Doomed. Autumn felt doomed.

* * *

Sean didn't get very far before he had to pull his truck to the side of the road and thrust the gearshift into park. Not because he needed to let the coffee cool a bit before sampling it. And not because he was still too drowsy to be driving. And not because he wanted to admire the way the sunrise was smudging the purple sky with fingers of orange and pink, either.

No, much to his amazement, it was because he had to try and get a grip on himself and his feelings.

It was the strangest thing. Not only had he never had to get a grip on himself for anything, but he'd never had feelings like the ones that were spiraling through him now. Strangest of all was that he soon came to realize he wasn't likely to get a grip on either his feelings or himself anytime soon. How could he, when he couldn't even identify what he was feeling to begin with?

Well, other than this weird sense of doom, anyway…

Just what the hell had happened back there at Autumn's bakery? he wondered, not for the first time since fleeing it in fear for his life—well, his social life, at any rate—less than half an hour ago. He'd entered thinking to do no more than ask her out on a date and had exited feeling as if he'd been struck by lightning.

He took a moment to replay every word the two of them had exchanged and to reconsider every suggestive comment he'd made. He recalled every look they'd shared, every sidelong glance they'd sneaked. But he couldn't figure out where, exactly, things between them had gotten so…hot. Somewhere along the line, though, the two of them had ceased to indulge in harmless banter and had become overcharged with…what? He still couldn't quite figure it out. And even weirder than all that…

He sighed his disbelief when he remembered. Even weirder than all that, Autumn Pulaski had refused to go out with him. *Had refused to go out with him.* Him! Sean Monahan! It was inconceivable. Impossible. Unthinkable.

Unacceptable.

Because Sean decided then and there that he would *not* accept her refusal. And not just because he had a point to prove to his brother Finn, either. But because there was something immediate and intense—not to mention hot and heavy—burning up the air between him and Autumn. And Sean just wasn't the kind of guy to let something like that go unexplored. Especially when there was a beautiful, desirable, sexy, cinnamon-scented, luscious, mouthwatering…uh…where was he? Oh, yeah. Especially when there was a woman like Autumn at the heart of it. And especially when that woman's eyes told him she was every bit as aware as he was of the strange fire burning between them.

So she'd said she wouldn't go out with him on Wednesday, had she? Well, then. Sean would just have to go back and ask her what she was doing on Tuesday instead. Then he remembered what *he* would be doing Tuesday. What the whole town of Marigold, Indiana, would be doing on Tuesday. What Autumn Pulaski would no doubt be doing on Tuesday, too. Because Tuesday was the Fourth of July. And everybody who was anybody in Marigold would be at the Annual Independence Day Picnic in Gardencourt Park. It was practically a requirement of citizenship.

Throwing his truck back into gear, Sean smiled. Yep, Tuesday would be a very good day for seeing Autumn again. Somehow he could just feel it in his bones. Their destinies were about to collide, for sure. And he couldn't help but thank his lucky stars for that.

Three

———

Sean found Autumn precisely where he'd known she would be on Tuesday, right smack in the middle of Gardencourt Park, at the Autumn's Harvest bread booth, hawking her wares. The Fourth of July was a very big deal in Marigold, Indiana, and pretty much the entire town closed down and showed up to celebrate it. Many of the local retailers, however, opened booths at the picnic, alongside the local craftspeople and artisans, selling specialty items or products that commemorated the day. Autumn, for example, he noticed as he approached the booth, was offering cranberry scones, white chocolate and macadamia nut cookies, and blueberry muffins—presumably in honor of Old Glory.

And he was glad he'd dressed up for the occasion in unripped, only marginally faded blue jeans and navy polo shirt, because Autumn, looking quite fetching, was dressed in what he, with his very limited knowledge of history—

Rory was, after all, the historian in the family—assumed must be Betsy Ross attire. Except that ol' Betsy probably hadn't filled out her Colonial garb quite the same way Autumn did. The full skirt of her multicolored, vertically striped gown flared nicely over her hips, and the top part hugged her generous breasts with *much* affection.

So affectionately, in fact, that had it not been for the white apron loosely covering her torso, the picnic would no doubt have had to be called on account of mass licentiousness. But the little mobcap perched atop Autumn's head went a long way toward tempering what Sean had decided was just her naturally sexy state.

Well, to the casual observer, the mobcap tempered her sexuality, anyway. Sean himself found the lacy little ruffled number to be surprisingly arousing. Then again, Autumn could be dressed up as George Washington's faithful springer spaniel, Buddy, and Sean would still find her attractive. Then again, maybe that wasn't an admission he should be owning up to. Still, she did look extremely delicious—or, rather, her baked goods looked extremely delicious—so what else could Sean do but step up to the booth and ask to sample her—or, rather, them?

"Excuse me, miss? I'll have one of those plump, luscious-looking scones, please," he announced, proud of himself for completing the request without a trace of suggestiveness.

Autumn's head had been bent when he approached, but she snapped it up quickly at the sound of his voice. Immediately she blushed, something Sean considered to be a very good sign, then her lips parted fractionally in clear surprise. "I...what?" she asked.

He jabbed a finger toward the rich bounty of baked goods before him. "I'd like a scone, please," he said, reading the hand-lettered sign in front of the selection. Otherwise he would have had to call it "one of those big lumpy things with the red spots,'' because he had no idea what a scone actually was. He just hoped the letter *c* in the word was a hard *c* and not a soft *c,* otherwise, he'd just made a fool of himself. Then again, maybe that was why she was looking at him the way she was looking at him—as if she weren't sure what language he was speaking.

He was about to correct himself—he hoped—and repeat his request, asking for a ''sone'' this time—or, at the very least, a ''big, lumpy thing with red spots''—when Autumn blinked twice, something that seemed to break whatever spell she'd fallen under.

''Right,'' she said. ''A scone.''

Sean breathed a silent sigh of relief when she pronounced it the same way he had. Then he expelled a soft groan of frustration as he watched her lean forward to collect a particularly fat one from the front of the pile—because when she did so, her apron fell forward a bit, offering him a view he was certain Betsy Ross never would have offered, even for the sake of her country. Then, as quickly as it had been given, that view disappeared, because Autumn straightened to drop the scone into a small paper bag.

When she extended it toward him, Sean was reminded of the last time he'd seen her, three mornings ago, when she'd thrust forward the cup of coffee he'd requested. This was becoming a habit, he thought, her pushing something his way in a silent sort of ''Beat it.''

''Here you go,'' she said brightly. A little too brightly, Sean thought. Translated, her words almost certainly meant, ''Beat it.'' Especially since she punctuated the statement with, ''That'll be $1.50, please.''

He held her gaze steadily as he tugged his wallet from the back pocket of his blue jeans and withdrew two faded bills, trading them for the little paper sack. When she turned to make his change, Sean allowed his gaze to rove over the back of her, finding it every bit as enticing as the front.

The flair of her hips and the dip of her waist gave new definition to the phrase *hourglass figure,* because he realized he wanted to take a whole lot of time exploring that part of her anatomy. Unfortunately, she chose that moment to spin back around with his change, and it was only at the last possible moment that Sean managed to drag his gaze back up again.

Oops. Okay, so maybe he hadn't dragged it back up *quite* soon enough, he was forced to concede when he saw Autumn scowling at him. But she was blushing again, too, and that made him smile. If she was blushing, it must mean she was uneasy, and if she was uneasy, it must mean she was having a reaction to him. He still wasn't entirely sure what *kind* of reaction she might be having, but at this point any reaction—short of throwing things—was welcome. And he was reasonably optimistic that her reaction now was something in the *good* family. After all, she *hadn't* thrown anything, had she?

"Have lunch with me," he said suddenly, impulsively, even though he had approached the booth with the express purpose of asking her to join him in that very activity. But he'd planned to go about it a bit less impulsively and a bit more smoothly. He hadn't meant to just blurt it out that way. He'd intended to work up to it gradually, because Autumn seemed like the kind of woman who needed a lot of buttering up.

Immediately Sean wished he'd come up with another way to put that. Because the thought of buttering up Autumn Pulaski—or whip creaming her up or chocolate saucing her up or maple syruping her up or honeying her up— just roused images that were far too graphic for a public, family-oriented place. Much better to entertain ideas like that later, when the two of them were alone together somewhere. Preferably somewhere that was close to a kitchen.

"Thank you, Mr. Monahan," she said as she handed him

his change, sounding a bit breathless for some reason, "but I'm much too busy to be able to break for lunch. As you can see, I'm womaning the booth all by myself."

As if cued by her announcement, two teenage girls dressed in huge khaki shorts and even larger white T-shirts bearing the Autumn's Harvest logo approached the table and ducked behind it. Each donned an apron identical to Autumn's, then each positioned herself at opposite sides of the booth.

"Thanks for the break, Autumn," said the blondest of the two. "Go ahead and grab some lunch yourself. Brittany and I can handle things here for a while. You deserve a break."

Autumn's cheeks pinked even more becomingly, and involuntarily Sean's smile grew broader. "Gosh, guess you'll have time, after all, won't you?" he asked.

"Uh," she replied eloquently. "I, um... Actually, I... That is, I need to... Ah..."

"Excellent," he said. "I know just the place."

Before she could object, he reached across the table to curl his fingers gently around her upper arm, silently urging her body—if not her spirit—toward the space between two tables that obviously served as an entry to the booth. Autumn stammered a few more half-formed—and, he was certain, halfhearted—protests, but Sean easily disregarded and dismissed each one. He kept talking until the two of them were a solid twenty or thirty yards from the booth, then, still not convinced he had her completely in his thrall—go figure—he looped his arm through hers and pulled her closer still. And all the while, Autumn seemed to be too flummoxed to do anything but follow him wherever he might lead her.

Now if he could just keep her flummoxed for two lunar months, Sean thought, he would make Finn eat his dare.

Unfortunately for Sean, though, by the time he'd picked

up two box lunches for them at the Rotarians' booth, snagged a couple of lemonades from the Girl Scouts' booth, and reached the fountain at the heart of Gardencourt Park— the nauseatingly romantic one that looked like an urn full of flowers spewing water all over a bunch of buck-naked cupids—Autumn was becoming decidedly less flummoxed. And damned if she didn't dig in her heels and tug her arm free of his, just as he deposited their lunches and lemonades on a two-seater wrought-iron bench that sat near a privacy-providing sweep of wisteria tumbling completely uninhibited—and almost blindingly purple—from a fat hedge behind it.

"Mr. Monahan," she began a bit breathlessly.

"Sean," he hastily corrected her, reaching out to wrap his fingers lightly around her wrist once more.

"*Mr. Monahan,*" she repeated adamantly. She deftly maneuvered her arm to her side before he could grasp it, curled both fists ineffectually—and really rather adorably, Sean thought—at her sides and frowned. "I'm afraid I can't accommodate your request right now. I have other things I should be doing besides eating lunch."

"Sean," he corrected her again. "I'm *Sean.* If you keep calling me 'Mr. Monahan,' you're going to have me *and* all four of my brothers heeding your beck and call."

The possibility of such a development seemed to make her feel queasy for some reason. "Oh, dear," she murmured. But she said nothing more to enlighten him about her state of uneasiness, just looked a little pale and distressed.

Sean found her reaction odd. There were plenty of women in Marigold who would jump at the chance to have the interest—romantic or otherwise—of the Monahan brothers, in just about any number or combination. Autumn Pulaski, however, evidently considered such attention to be a fate worse than death.

"Sean," he said for a third time, feeling frustrated for no reason he could name. "Call me Sean. Please."

He couldn't imagine why, but he really, really wanted to hear her say his name out loud. Maybe it was because she had one of those husky, breathy voices, the kind most men only heard when they were sitting in a dark movie theater listening to Kathleen Turner or Demi Moore or Debra Winger in Dolby stereo. The kind of voice that made even the simplest statement sound like an intimate suggestion, somehow, and turned a man's name into a sensual promise.

When Autumn opened her mouth to speak, Sean braced himself for the sexual awakening he was sure would follow. But instead of uttering his name in that deep, smooth, languid way, she said, "I really should get back to the booth."

"Why?" he asked. "Your employees looked more than capable of handling the crowd—which, incidentally, is thinning as we speak, because the lunch hour is drawing to a close—and it doesn't sound like you've had lunch yet yourself."

"I've been snacking all morning," she assured him. "It's one of the perks of the job. With all those snacks, I don't need any lunch."

He threw her his most salacious smile, dropped his eyelids to half-mast and adopted what he'd been told more than once was a very sexy demeanor. Mostly this involved hooking both hands on his hips, shifting his weight to one foot, flexing his pecs and biceps and tossing his head back with just a touch of arrogance. Okay, so that last part was more because his hair was in his eyes and in need of a trim, but it still went a long way toward completing the sexy demeanor thing—Sean was sure of it.

"Snacking," he then began coyly, "is not the same thing as lunching, Autumn. When one snacks, one never completely satisfies one's...hunger, does one, even if one snacks frequently? I mean, a little nibble here, a little nibble there... It's never quite enough, is it?''

He took a single, leisurely step forward, bringing his body to within inches of hers. But he didn't touch her, didn't so much as reach for her, only continued to keep her gaze pinned with his own. And my, what a warm gaze hers was, too, he noted. There was no question that he had her full attention.

"Oh, sure," he continued softly, growing a little warmer himself as he watched her, "snacks can be more... provocative. More...arousing. You get variety. You get a little taste of something exotic, something you might not normally...have. And there's just something so tempestuous about the haste and the immediacy and the secrecy of a snack, isn't there?" he added, dropping his voice to a level only she would be able to hear. "Snacks can be very titillating, Autumn, because they're somehow more forbidden.

"But *lunch*," he continued, wrapping his voice around the word in the same smooth way he curled his fingers loosely around her wrist to pull her body closer still, "is much more fulfilling. It requires greater commitment, greater attention to detail."

He tugged her gently forward, until her body was flush with his, and waited for her to protest. But instead of protesting, she only opened one hand over his chest, splaying her fingers over his heart. And Sean could see by the way the pulse at the base of her throat leaped at the contact that her own heartbeat was every bit as rapid, as ragged, as his own.

"One takes one's time with lunch," he told her even more softly, his voice a scant whisper now. "Lunch is so much more satisfying. There are so many ways to enjoy it, and there's so much to consume." He dipped his head to very lightly nuzzle her temple, reveling in the little gasp of shock—and dare he say delight?—that escaped her at the contact. "You have to go slowly with lunch, Autumn," he continued, his mouth right beside her ear now. "You have to be more thorough, taste everything you have on your plate. And you know, done correctly, lunch is infinitely more...pleasurable...than snacking."

As much as he wanted to duck his head more and drag his open mouth along the elegant curve of her neck, somehow Sean found the strength to draw himself away. He didn't go far, however, and he dropped one hand to the graceful curve of her hip. Again he prepared himself to be rebuffed, but Autumn offered no reaction one way or the other. When he'd pulled back far enough to gaze at her face, he saw that she was studying him with great preoccupation, even though he'd finished his dissertation on the different manners of...satisfying oneself.

Strangely enough, though, her attention seemed to be focused almost entirely on his mouth. A tremor of something hot and volatile shook him when he realized it, then nearly exploded when he saw how her pupils had grown larger, her cheeks more rosy, and how her lips had parted softly, as if she wasn't—quite—getting enough breath.

She wasn't the only one, he thought. Suddenly Sean felt a bit dizzy himself, as if the oxygen to his brain had been momentarily blocked. Then again, who needed oxygen when you had a woman like Autumn gazing at you like that? Suddenly even lunch didn't seem like enough to satisfy him. Because over the past couple of moments, he had grown hungry to the point of being ravenous, and he wasn't sure there was enough food on the planet to sate him.

Of course, food was the last thing on his mind right now. Because Autumn Pulaski was looking at him as if she wanted to tuck a cherry into his mouth and flambé him. And he realized that, at that moment, there was nothing in life that would have brought him greater joy than being, well…cherry flambéed. By Autumn Pulaski. This very second.

Oh, man.

It was happening again, he thought. That same strange electricity that had shuddered between them in the bakery that morning had returned, charging the air between them once more. And what had begun as a well orchestrated, carefully rehearsed flirtation had been jerked completely out of Sean's hands.

"Um, yeah, okay," she said softly. "Lunch sounds, uh…pretty good. I, uh…I could go for some, um, lunch. I guess."

Oh, she was just so cute when she was flummoxed, Sean thought. But he said nothing, just closed his fingers more snugly around her wrist and guided her to the bench, where he had strategically placed their lunches in such a fashion as to require them to sit *very* close to each other when they took their seats. It was a fact that Autumn duly noted, because before sitting down, she rearranged everything to construct a makeshift wall between their two designated places, perching herself primly on one side of it, nodding in silent invitation for Sean to take his seat on the other side.

Damn.

Squelching a sigh of defeat, he acquiesced with as much good grace as he could and reached for his own lunch. The new moon wasn't until tomorrow, he reminded himself. That gave him another full day to woo Autumn and convince her that she should give him a chance.

Another day, he remembered, *and* another night.

How Autumn let herself get talked into things sometimes, she really would never be able to understand. Then again, Sean Monahan hadn't given her much choice had he? Not only had he practically seduced her earlier that afternoon—right there in front of the Gertrude Hepplewhite Memorial Fountain, no less—just by explaining the differences between snacking and lunching, but he'd followed her around all day like an eager-to-be-accepted puppy.

He had virtually haunted the Autumn's Harvest booth all afternoon while she worked, had smiled that heart-tugging, heat-seeking smile of his, had twinkled those devastating blue eyes, had been more enchanting than any fairy-tale prince could ever hope to be. She hadn't been able to resist him. He'd just been so…so handsome. So…charming. So…eligible. And then, before she realized what was happening…

Autumn sighed restlessly. Before she realized what was happening, she found herself stretched out alongside him on a faded, flowered quilt beneath the stars, her entire body humming with anticipation at the prospect of the fireworks that were bound to explode any minute.

Fortunately, those fireworks would be literal, not figurative, because a good foot of faded, flowered quilt lay between her and Sean, and very soon, the first burst of rockets would light the sky above Marigold to open the annual Fourth of July fireworks display. Literal fireworks, Autumn repeated to herself adamantly. *Not* figurative ones.

At least, she thought further, reconsidering, she hoped there wouldn't be any figurative fireworks tonight. Sean was, after all, so handsome. So charming. So eligible.

Stop it right there, Autumn, she instructed herself firmly. There would *not* be any figurative fireworks tonight. Or *any* night, for that matter. Of that—if nothing else—she was completely certain. Because if there was one thing she had learned since leaving Chicago to come to Marigold, it was how to turn fireworks into fizzle in no time flat. She hadn't experienced *any* fireworks since her arrival here, not with *anybody*. She hadn't even come close to the merest spark. In fact, there hadn't been the least little smolder of *anything* with *any* man for more than two years. And by golly, Autumn had no intention of setting fire to any wicks tonight. She didn't care if it was the Fourth of July. Sean Monahan could just keep his sparkler to himself.

"Sparkler?" he piped up suddenly, softly, his voice much, much too close for her comfort.

She jackknifed into a sitting position, then whipped her head around in time to see that Sean was sitting up now, too. And he was accepting not one, but two, sparklers from a young woman who appeared to be passing them out through the crowd. He extended one toward Autumn, and she shook her head quickly.

"No," she said, just as hastily. "No, thank you. No sparkler. I, um, I'm not much one for fireworks."

He arched a single dark brow in response, though whether the gesture was an indication of his skepticism, his curiosity or his speculation, she wasn't sure. "No fireworks?" he repeated.

"None," she said firmly. "Not ever."

Now he gaped softly in clear disbelief. "Never?"

"Never."

"Are you serious?" he asked, seeming shocked by the notion for some reason. "You mean you've never in your life…you know…lit one off?"

Autumn squirmed a little anxiously. "Well, I didn't say *that*," she qualified reluctantly. "I've experienced fireworks. Once or twice. Just not lately, that's all. Not for a while now."

He eyed her with much consideration. "How long is 'not for a while now'?" he asked.

She shrugged as she tried to recall… Oh, yes. Now she remembered. More's the pity. The last time she'd experienced fireworks had been two weeks before her alleged wedding to Stanley, when they'd gone to New Orleans for Mardi Gras. "About two and a half years ago," she said.

This time Sean dropped his mouth open wide, very obviously appalled by the revelation. "You haven't indulged in any fireworks for *two and a half years?*"

She shook her head slowly and wondered absently if they were talking about the same thing. But Autumn hadn't been in Marigold for the Fourth of July last year—she'd been at a baker's conference in Indianapolis—and the year before that, she'd had a sinus infection and wasn't able to make the local celebration. So this was definitely her first fireworks display for some time.

Finally, "No-o-o," she said slowly, reassuring him. "It's been more than two years, for sure."

He gaped even wider. "Are you *serious?*"

She felt indignant for some reason, though she couldn't imagine why. "Of course I'm serious."

He contemplated her silently for a moment, then asked, "Not even like…a smoke bomb?"

Autumn expelled a soft sound of disapproval. "No, not even a smoke bomb."

He studied her for a moment longer. "Not even a firecracker?" he asked.

"Certainly not."

He shook his head slowly, as if in disappointment. "Man. And here I was planning to light up a whole mess of bottle rockets before the night was over."

She lifted her chin primly. "Well, you'll have to do it without me."

"Jeez, where's the fun in that?" he asked. "I mean, yeah, there's a certain sort of forbidden pleasure in setting them off alone, but…" He leaned even closer, his expression shadowed by the darkness, now that the sun had dipped completely behind the trees. "But it's so much more fun with a friend," he finished, his voice low and seductive, his breath warm and erotic against her neck.

Autumn swallowed hard and tried not to notice how

good he smelled, like moonlight and warm summer evening and something wonderfully elusive and masculine. "Sean…" she said, deliberately lacing the word with warning.

Instead of a cautious reaction, however, he leaned back on one elbow and stretched his legs out alongside hers. Although their bodies weren't touching, he seemed much too close, and she fancied she could feel his heat mingling with her own.

"I like how you say my name," he told her softly. "I like it a lot."

A hot, tautly strung wire hummed somewhere deep inside her, making Autumn feel a bit like a bottle rocket herself. A bottle rocket that was *this close* to igniting. "Why are you doing this?" she asked suddenly, uncertain, really, when she'd decided to ask.

"Doing what?" he replied with what was clearly feigned innocence.

"Why have you been following me around all day, making everything you say sound like a come-on?"

"Have I been doing that?"

"You know you have."

He eyed her intently for a moment before answering. "Maybe I just want to get to know you better," he finally said.

"Why?"

He shrugged, but there was nothing careless in the gesture. "Gee, let me think on that a minute." He proceeded to do just that—though, clearly, he wasn't thinking all that hard. Because after less than a minute he continued, "It *might* be because you're an incredibly beautiful, extraordinarily interesting woman. Though, mind you, that's just a shot in the dark."

Although Autumn didn't believe him on either count, she

couldn't help blushing at his frankness. "You, uh...you think I'm interesting?" she said.

"Oh, you bet," he assured her.

"Most people in Marigold think I'm an oddball."

He smiled at that, but there was nothing patronizing in his expression at all. "I prefer to think of you as more of a free spirit," he told her.

Just like that, the bubble of happiness that had begun to effervesce inside Autumn went *pop. Free spirit,* she repeated dismally to herself. In other words, she further translated, *Oddball.* "Oh," she said flatly. "I see."

She really did hate being Marigold's resident "free spirit," and she still wasn't sure what she'd said or done to be awarded the moniker by the local citizenry. All right, so maybe "Autumn" was kind of an unusual name, but she hadn't chosen it for herself, had she? No. Her parents had been the ones to call her that. And Autumn did like her name, even if it was a bit unconventional. Still, that didn't make her an oddball.

And all right, so she favored loosely fitting dresses in natural fabrics and Birkenstock sandals, and she let her hair grow naturally as it would, and she shunned cosmetics, and she grew herbs in her backyard, and she practiced yoga every day. That still didn't make her a free spirit. Lots of people did those things. And lots of people read the *Tao Te Ching* every morning. And lots of people followed the recommendations of their astrologers. And lots of people were vegetarians. And lots of people liked listening to the mating calls of the blue whale when they were alone at night to help them sleep. That didn't make Autumn an oddball, either.

Not to her way of thinking, anyway. To the residents of Marigold, Indiana, however...

"There's no shame in being a free spirit, Autumn," Sean said quietly. "If you want to know the truth, I envy you your ability to totally disregard what everyone thinks or says about you.''

She lifted her chin fractionally, but couldn't quite meet his gaze. ''Who says I disregard what everyone thinks or says about me?'' she asked softly.

When she braved a glance at him, she realized he had opened his mouth to respond. But no words emerged to give her any hint as to what he might be thinking. Before he had a chance to answer, the fireworks—literal ones, thankfully—began, spraying the night sky with bright bits of blue and red and yellow and green, and anything she or Sean might have said was lost in the ''Oohs'' and ''Aahs'' of the crowd surrounding them. Autumn was no more immune to the spectacle than anyone else was, and she quickly became captivated by the display. Sean, too, seemed to succumb, because eventually he stopped looking at her and gazed up at the night sky instead. And only then was she able to really relax and enjoy herself.

And that enjoyment lasted right up until the last kaleidoscopic burst of color dissolved into the black night and the final boom of manufactured thunder faded. After that, though, Autumn's pleasure ebbed, because that was when everyone around her and Sean began to gather up their things and head home. And that was when she realized she had no idea what to do next.

She'd closed the bread booth some time ago, and Sean had helped her and her employees pack everything in her aged and battered VW Microbus. *But* lots *of people drove VW Microbuses,* she had told him when he'd eyed her mode of transportation with much interest. *And* lots *of people put crazy daisies and a big peace sign on the front.* Now there was nothing left for her to do but gather up her faded, flowered quilt—and what was left of the parmesan rosemary loaf they had shared—and carry those, too, back to her van. Then she could say good night—or, rather, goodbye—to Sean Monahan and hope like heaven that she never saw him this up-close-and personal again.

She proceeded to do just that, but Sean intercepted her, snatching up the quilt and folding it over and over and over, his gaze never once leaving hers. "I'll help you," he said unnecessarily.

"Really, Sean, that's not necess—"

"And I'll walk you to your…to that thing you drive," he said with another one of those all-too-charming smiles. When he saw that she was going to decline, he hastily added, "Hey, you can't be too careful."

She couldn't quite squelch the chuckle that erupted at that. "And *you* can't be serious."

He shrugged a bit apologetically. "Okay, so it's not exactly dangerous to walk the streets—or parks—of Marigold alone," he conceded. His smile turned roguish, and heat splashed through Autumn's midsection. "It's not much fun to walk the streets or parks alone. I could keep you company," he offered boyishly.

Oh, could he, she thought. He could keep her company for a long, long, *long* ti—

"Really, Sean, that's not necess—"

"What are you doing tomorrow night?" he asked suddenly, cutting off her protest—again—before she could complete it.

Honestly, the change of subject was so fast, Autumn nearly got whiplash. "I…I…I told you," she stammered. "I…I…I'm working."

"Only up until nine," he reminded her.

"All the way until nine," she corrected him.

But he clearly wasn't going to take no for an answer. Because he persisted "What are you doing after nine?"

"I'm going home," she told him succinctly.

His smile broadened. "I could meet you there."

Oh. Dear.

"Um, I don't think that's a good idea," she told him.

"Then I could meet you somewhere else," he offered.

Autumn sighed. Clearly he intended to go out with her. Clearly, nothing she said would put him off. Clearly, he wasn't going to leave her alone until she said yes. Clearly, she was going to have to…date him.

And clearly, she realized, something about that realization made her feel very, very warm inside.

"All right," she finally told him, knowing she was making a mistake, but helpless to do anything but agree. "I'll meet you somewhere else. Just tell me where."

Four

——

Had she realized that Sean Monahan was going to suggest the Skyway Drive-In for their…assignation…Autumn almost certainly would not have agreed to go out with him. But he had made some very valid points when suggesting the location. Not the least of which was that, since she was working until nine and had to clean herself up a bit afterward, they wouldn't arrive anywhere until nearly ten. And by ten o'clock most places in Marigold were winding down, and many had already closed. That pretty much left them with three choices.

They could go to Autumn's place.

They could go to Sean's placc.

Or they could go to the Skyway Drive-In.

It hadn't taken very sophisticated decision-making skills for Autumn to choose the place she thought best. Or, at the very least, the place she thought safest. Especially when one took into consideration the fact that the Skyway's dou-

ble feature that night was *The Incredible Mr. Limpet* and
the original *That Darn Cat.* There was nothing like a combination of Don Knotts and Hayley Mills to squelch any
potential for hanky-panky. Of that, Autumn was confident.

At least, of that she *had* been confident. Earlier. Before
Sean had rolled his Jeep Cherokee—the one with the really
big back seat—into an isolated parking place at the back
of the drive-in, where it was very, very dark and very, very
unpopulated and very, very secluded and very, very romantic. And although he'd attached the speaker to the lowered driver's side window, he'd adjusted the volume to the
soft romantic murmur setting. He'd also lowered the rest
of the Jeep's windows, and now a nice warm—romantic—
breeze rolled through, nudging a few flyaway strands of
Autumn's hair that had escaped the braid she hadn't had
time to repair.

And although she knew she was still redolent of freshly
baked bread, she supposed there were worse things a person
could smell like upon finishing one's shift at work. She
had, at least, had time to change her clothes, opting for a
white cotton dress styled after a Victorian petticoat. She
supposed she was a bit overdressed, but she'd had no idea
what to wear to a drive-in movie, having never visited one
before. Sean, she noted, looked cool and casual in jeans
that were only marginally faded and a short-sleeved oxford-
cloth shirt that was about two shades deeper blue than his
eyes—which meant it was very blue indeed. Not that she
could see his eyes in the darkness, of course, but she could
remember them all too well.

Boy, could she remember. And had on several occasions
over the past twenty-four hours. Both consciously and un-
consciously. In fact, her dreams the night before had become so graphic at one point that Autumn had awoken
feeling hot and agitated and curiously in need of,

well…lighting something up. Setting off some fireworks. It was the oddest thing.

All in all, she decided, the current mood—both in Sean's Jeep and in Autumn's mind—was much too romantic for a first date. But she had no idea how to rectify that. Short of leaping out the passenger side door and fleeing into the night, which, though certainly effective, would have been frightfully impolite.

Oh, why had she agreed to let him pick her up at home?

She turned to find that Sean had leaned back comfortably in his seat and was eyeing her with what she could only liken to serious intent. And suddenly that fleeing into the night, regardless of its being such a social no-no, was beginning to look rather good.

"I'm sorry about the movie selection," he said, grinning sheepishly. "I could have sworn the double feature tonight was something else."

Autumn wasn't sure she should speculate on what that *something else* might be. Sean Monahan seemed like the kind of guy who would look forward to a double feature of *Thong Bikini Beach* and *Sorority Slumber Party*. Then again, this *was* Marigold, Indiana, and Autumn was reasonably certain that such films would *never* show up at the Skyway.

"This is fine," she assured him, hoping lightning didn't strike her for that one. She further lied, "I'm a big Don Knotts fan from way, way back."

He looked vaguely horrified by the admission, but Autumn decided not to own up to the falsehood. Maybe it would serve as an effective deterrent in keeping him on his side of the Jeep.

"Yeah, well, I'll grant you that Barney Fife is, arguably, the precedent for goofiness by which industry standards should be defined but…" He shrugged philosophically. "I just never did get that whole 'Apple Dumpling Gang' thing.''

Autumn smiled. ''It wasn't one of his best performances,'' she conceded.

After that stellar opening, the conversation lagged a bit— go figure—until Sean offered to brave the crowds in a quest for popcorn. Anything to alleviate the tension that had settled over them, Autumn thought, watching him go. Honestly. She still couldn't figure out what the two of them were doing here, still didn't understand why Sean Monahan had asked her out in the first place. Thinking back, it was almost as if the only reason he'd come into the bakery Saturday morning had been to ask her out, despite his assurance that all he'd wanted was a cup of coffee.

He'd been so insistent about asking her out, too, as if his life and livelihood depended on seeing her socially. It made no sense. She'd lived in Marigold for more than two years now, quite nicely, thanks, without the intervention of any of the Monahan brothers. Then, suddenly, there was Sean, the most dangerous of the bunch, as far as Autumn was concerned, demanding that she go out with him.

And, of course, she hadn't been able to resist him. He was too handsome, too charming and too eligible. Now she was going to have to make it through a full lunar month with him. But just how was she supposed to manage that?

Then another thought struck her. He did know about her rule, didn't he? He must. *Everyone* in Marigold knew about her rule. Didn't they? Surely Sean wasn't working under the mistaken impression that the two of them would be dating for longer than four weeks. Was he? Then again, it might not hurt to broach the subject when he got back, just to make certain they were both clear on the matter. She didn't want there to be any kind of misunderstanding. Because she absolutely would *not* be dating Sean for more than four weeks. That was all there was too it.

Autumn knew her no-dating-for-longer-than-a-lunar-month rule was a contributing factor—perhaps, ultimately, even the defining factor—in Marigold's assessment of her as an oddball. But she couldn't help it. What else was she supposed to do? Ever since moving to her newly adopted hometown, she'd had to fend off invitations from the local bachelors. Not that she kidded herself that she was any great catch, or thoroughly irresistible to the opposite sex. *Au contraire.* But a single, feminine newcomer to Marigold was, evidently, considered to be something of an occasion, and quite a few of her new male neighbors had expressed an unmistakable interest in her.

But Autumn had learned the hard way that her judgment, when it came to men, was, to put it mildly, Very Bad. Clearly, she could not tell the good ones from the bad ones, because she kept getting involved with, well, losers. Men who promised her the moon and gave her a dirt cloud instead. What was the saying? Once burned, twice shy? As far as she was concerned, twice burned, *always* shy. She wasn't about to be left at the altar—literally—a third time. Ergo, she couldn't afford to get involved with anyone of the male persuasion, period. So, shortly after her arrival in Marigold, she had concocted a plan that would prohibit a repeat of the painful experiences she'd suffered in the past.

Autumn had adopted a rule, a hard-and-fast one, that she simply would not date any man for any length of time that might lead to something more substantial than mere casual dating. She'd figured that the average couple took about a month to get to know each other well, and that after that month things either fizzled between them or progressed to something more serious. Autumn didn't want serious. She wanted fizzle. So one month seemed like a viable period for dating any individual male, without there being any risk of deep, emotional involvement.

But some months were longer than other months, she'd

been forced to realize. And all modesty aside, she'd had to consider the possibility that a February boyfriend might feel cheated because he wasn't given as much dating time as, say, an August boyfriend. Even in a leap year, there would have been some disparity. Therefore, she'd decided that a lunar month, which was always four weeks long, regardless, would be a much more equitable time frame to work with. Hey, who would be able to complain then, huh? she'd told herself. It was a perfectly good plan.

Except for its being kind of odd.

But then, she was the resident oddball, wasn't she? Autumn had reminded herself. She'd figured that out almost immediately after moving to Marigold. She hadn't missed the talk. She hadn't missed the looks. She hadn't missed the helpless sighs, followed by the pats on the hand. She knew her fellow Marigoldians all thought of her as an oddball. So no one was really surprised by her rule, once she put voice to it. Ultimately it had turned out to be a flawless plan.

And if there was the occasional man who took exception to it, well… He got over it. Eventually. Autumn wasn't so egotistical that she feared she broke hearts. She knew she didn't. It was that simple. And, better still, she hadn't had her own heart broken, either.

Not yet, anyway.

The thought erupted in her brain with a most unwelcome echo, and she wondered why. Sean Monahan was no different from any of the other men she had dated since coming to Marigold, she told herself. Just because he was handsome. Just because he was charming. Just because he was eligible. She'd dated a number of comparable men—well, pretty comparable; the Monahans were, after all, a fairly exceptional bunch—and hadn't once come close to losing her heart. It would only be for four weeks.

And it would be fun, she told herself. She hadn't dated

much over the last several lunar months, and she was getting tired of her solitude. There was no way she would fall in love with Sean in such a short span of time, she further assured herself. Love was much too important an emotion for it to be fashioned in only four weeks' time. She hadn't come close to falling in love with any of the other men she had dated in Marigold. And Sean was no different from any of them, not really. He wasn't. Truly. To be sure. Honest. She wasn't risking anything by dating him for four weeks.

She hoped.

The movie was well underway by the time Sean returned. Though, somehow, Autumn deduced he wasn't all that bothered by having missed the beginning. When he set a massive tub of popcorn on the seat between them, she viewed it with a response that was rather mixed. On one hand she was relieved to have some barrier—however ineffectual—placed between them. On the other hand she was irritated to have some barrier—however ineffectual—placed between them.

Oh, stop, she admonished herself. This was all for the best, and she knew it. The slower things went with Sean, the better. The more barriers—effective or otherwise—that went up between them, the more assurances she'd have that their relationship wouldn't go too far.

Whoa, she thought. *Rewind.* Scratch that *relationship* business. There was no relationship. There would be no relationship. There would be only fun. There would be only a good time. Four weeks' worth of dating and nothing more. Just like always. It was, after all, her rule. Her single, irrefutable *rule.*

Unfortunately, when Sean reached behind the seat and plucked a bottle of red wine from the floor, Autumn's conviction in that department wavered some. This really was becoming much too romantic an affair. She squeezed her eyes shut tight at her choice of terms. Not an *affair,* she immediately contradicted herself. What this was becoming was much too romantic a…a…a *thing.* There. That word would suffice nicely.

"Nineteen eighty-three," he said as he held up the bottle, label forward, for her inspection. "A very good year for this particular grape."

Not that Autumn would have had a clue what to look for in a wine label—she was more of a wine cooler kind of gal herself—but she nodded her head in what she hoped he would interpret as her sage and very informed approval.

When he smiled in return, she was confident she had pulled off her pose reasonably well. And after completing another quick foray into the nether regions of the back seat, Sean produced two wineglasses and a corkscrew, then proceeded to make good use of all three. In no time at all, Autumn found herself cradling in her hand a long-stemmed, wide-bowled glass, half-filled with richly fragrant wine. Its flavor, too, when she tasted it, was robust and full-bodied, and it went down… She sighed her satisfaction as it splashed warmth through her belly. My, but that was really much too smooth.

When she turned to look at Sean, she found him smiling at her again, in that roguish, charming sort of way she had come to both anticipate and dread. Because when he smiled that way… She sighed again, more deeply this time, and with infinitely more satisfaction. Well. Suffice it to say, when he smiled that way, something inside her began to ebb and flow with the satin smoothness of the calmest sea. Where she would have thought such a smile would set off raucous alarm bells in her brain, instead, it made her feel more content than she ever had in her life.

"So…you like?" he asked, his voice moving over her like a soft caress in the otherwise silent car.

"Mmm," she told him. "It's lovely." Somehow,

though, she suspected he knew that she was talking about more than just the wine.

He hesitated only a moment before remarking, very softly, "No, the wine is savory. *You,* Autumn, are lovely."

Oh, my. Had she just been thinking she felt content? Actually, she was beginning to feel rather…well, the word *aroused* came to mind…

Oh, dear.

"Truly," Sean continued, his voice dipping even lower as stretched his arm across the back of her seat and began to lean close. "Lovely."

Autumn swallowed with some difficulty when she heard the unmistakably seductive croon, and she just couldn't quite make herself look away from his face. His incredibly handsome face, that was half bathed in shadow, half washed in what little light from the movie screen managed to make it back this far. For one brief, strangely delirious moment, she thought Sean intended to kiss her. And for one briefer, even more delirious moment, she realized how much she wanted him to.

In that instant Autumn could imagine all too well how soft and warm his mouth would be, how gently, perhaps even tentatively, he would brush his lips over hers, once, twice, maybe even three times. Then he might lift a hand to her face to drag his bent knuckles softly over her cheek and cup the other behind her neck to pull her closer still. Close enough to taste her deeply, touch her intimately and eventually…

In a last-ditch effort to save what little sanity she had left, Autumn quickly turned her attention to the movie. "Oh, look!" she cried, probably a bit louder than was actually necessary. "This is where the incredible Mr. Limpet turns into a fish. I *love* this part! Turn it up! Quick!" She scooped up a handful of popcorn, studiously avoided looking at Sean and, in between nibbles, added, "The special effects in this movie are *so* remarkable, considering the time when it was made.''

Sean was silent for a moment, and Autumn couldn't help but notice that he did not, in fact, turn up the volume as she had asked. What he did do was remove his arm from the back of her seat and return it to his side, and then grunt what sounded like a halfhearted agreement under his breath. Thankfully, though, he didn't press the change of subject. Instead he, too, reached into the tub of popcorn, leaned back in his seat with what she assured herself was *not* moroseness and contented himself with watching the movie.

For all of ten minutes.

Because once the novelty of the animated Mr. Limpet swimming around in the very real sea wore off, Sean turned to gaze at her once again.

"So. Autumn. Tell me about yourself," he said.

She shrugged off the question quite literally and sidestepped it by asking one of her own. "What's there to tell?"

"You tell me."

She braved a glimpse in his general direction. Her eyes had become accustomed to the darkness by now, so she could see him rather clearly. Really, too clearly. He was much too handsome. What on earth had she been thinking when she'd agreed to date him? Oh, yes. She remembered now. She hadn't been thinking at all. She'd just been feeling all warm and fuzzy and…stuff…inside.

"I-I-I'm not sure what you want to know," she said, congratulating herself for finally being honest with him about something.

"Everything," he said succinctly. Then, less succinctly, he added, "I want to know everything there is to know about you. Every last detail."

Oh, well, when he put it that way…

"All right, then. I was born in a small log cabin in the woods," she began.

"Very funny," he interjected dryly. "Come on. Tell me the real story."

She blinked at him, confused. "No, really," she assured him. "I was born in a small log cabin in the woods."

He eyed her dubiously.

"My parents—their names were Sunflower and Cumulus Pulaski—"

"Uh…Sunflower and Cumulus?" he interrupted.

"Well, you said you wanted to know every detail," she reminded him.

"Yeah, but…Sunflower and Cumulus?" he echoed.

"Well, Mom called Daddy Cume for short," she conceded. "Originally they were Susan Miller and Chris Pulaski, but when they exchanged their vows in a Haight-Ashbury park during the Summer of Love, they decided to legally change their names to Sunflower and Cumulus Pulaski. Of course, they never legally *married*," she added, "but then, who needs a piece of paper, when you have love in your heart, right?"

Sean sat silently for a moment, gazing at her, then said softly, "Um, yeah. Right. I guesso."

"Anyway," she continued blithely, "they built the log cabin themselves. When they went to Woodstock, they fell in love with New England and decided to stay in the area. They hitchhiked up to Maine and bought some land, then built their house from trees that my father hewed himself. Mom started a small herb and vegetable garden—all organically grown, naturally—and my father worked as a carpenter. They raised five children in that log cabin," she concluded wistfully. "Me, my sisters, Lavender and Aura, and my brothers, Storm and Chip."

"Chip?" Sean asked.

She nodded. "I loved that cabin. Mom and Dad still live there."

"And what about your brothers and sisters?"

"Oh, we've all scattered to the four winds," Autumn said, unable to conceal the melancholy that tinted her words, her feelings. "Lavender just graduated from the Air Force Academy, and Chip's a stockbroker, and Aura is an aeronautical engineer, and Storm is designing evening gowns for Givenchy."

Sean was still studying her with much skepticism when he asked, "Your father made enough as a carpenter to support a family of seven?"

"Well, Mom did grow most of our food. I did mention organically, didn't I?"

"Uh, yes. Yes, you did."

"And we had chickens and cows, too," Autumn elaborated. "And, of course, there was Mom's trust fund."

Sean's dark eyebrows shot up to nearly his hair line. "Her trust fund?"

Autumn nodded. "Her father—my grandfather?—is the founder and CEO of GTC. GlobalTechnic Computers. Maybe you've heard of them?"

Sean squeezed his eyes shut tight as he digested this new information about Autumn Pulaski. She was the grand-daughter of one of the wealthiest men in America? Ho, boy. "Um, yeah," he managed to say. "As would be the case with 99 percent of the planet's population, I've heard of GTC. So that would make you…an heiress?"

Her eyebrows arrowed downward as she considered his question, and something told Sean that this was the first time in her entire life that she'd actually ever given the concept much thought. "Hmm. Yes. I guess it would. How about that?"

How about that? he echoed to himself.

"So," she continued, completely oblivious to the fact

that she had just owned up to the fact that her family was worth millions and millions of dollars. "How about you? You come from a large family, too. That's something we have in common." She popped a few pieces of popcorn into her mouth and munched happily as she waited for Sean's reply.

"Um, yes. But my grandfather was a stonemason, not a technological pioneer. The Monahans, I'm afraid, are very firmly entrenched in Middle-Class America."

"Well, there's no shame in that," Autumn pointed out matter-of-factly. "Honest hard work garners the greatest rewards life has to offer."

Somehow he knew she was perfectly serious about that. Why else would she be working herself? Most people in her position would be perfectly content to remain idle and mooch off the family coffers, but the entire Pulaski clan, it appeared, preferred to work to earn their way. Sean thanked her parents for that, for instilling in their children the basics of the American Work Ethic. Otherwise, Autumn would be well and truly beyond his reach. There was no way he'd stand a chance with a high-society heiress. With a baker of bread, however, he felt right at home.

Then again, why did he care whether he stood a chance with her or not? All he planned to do was date Autumn for a couple of months and nothing more. Well, okay, maybe, you know...*deep down,* he had hopes of moving beyond the dating stage and into the physical stage. If Autumn were amenable to that, too. Sean had no intention of there being any more to their...to their...um, to their *thing*—whatever it was—than that.

Nevertheless he did feel right at home with her.

Too much at home, he realized. Because sitting here in the darkness of his Jeep with Autumn, watching a Don Knotts movie, for criminy's sake, really felt much too good. And even having known her for such a short time, he was completely comfortable with her. She was easy to talk to. She didn't make him feel awkward or uncertain the way many women had. Maybe that was because she didn't seem to have any expectations of him. And he couldn't decide yet whether that was a good thing or a bad thing.

"There's something we should get straight, up front," she said suddenly, her voice all seriousness now.

Okay, scratch that last part about expectations, Sean thought. Evidently, he'd been mistaken in that regard. Oddly, though, even in recognizing that, he still didn't feel awkward or uncertain around her.

"What's that?" he asked.

She said nothing for a moment, but seemed to be mulling over some matter of grave importance. Finally, slowly, as if she were taking great care in choosing her words, she said, "You do know about my rule, don't you?"

He smiled. Oh, *that*. "The lunar-month thing?" he asked.

She nodded as she released a breath that was unmistakably relieved. But she sounded a tad anxious as she added, very quickly, "Yes, the lunar-month thing. You realize that I never date a man for longer than four weeks, don't you? I mean, I don't want to be presumptuous or anything. Naturally, I don't assume that the two of us *will* necessarily be dating for that entire length of time, but we do seem to be dating—correct me if I'm wrong, of course, but I don't think I'm mistaken on that score—and I just wanted to make sure you knew up front about my rule, because I very much want to make clear that—"

"Oh, I think you can assume we'll be dating for that entire length of time, Autumn," Sean interjected mildly.

His assurance seemed to stump her, because she stopped speaking entirely. In fact, all she managed by way of a response was, "Oh."

"In fact," he continued. Then he thought better of it.

There was no need to voice his intention of dating her for longer than her lunar month. It would no doubt lead to trouble. Best to just take things a day at a time for now. Or a week at a time. Or a lunar month at a time. Whatever.

"In fact what?" she prodded.

But Sean only shook his head, thinking it might be best to keep his plan to himself for now. "Nothing," he told her. "Just..."

He hesitated for a moment, wondering where to go next with the conversation. Immediately, though, he knew where he wanted to take it. Because there was one question he very much wanted to ask her, one that just about everybody in Marigold, Indiana would probably want to know the answer to.

Feeling very cautious for some reason, Sean said, "So, Autumn. This lunar-month rule that you just described."

"And that you just agreed to," she hastily interjected.

Sean declined to comment on that. He'd agreed to no such thing. "This lunar-month rule," he began again.

"Yes?" she asked warily.

He donned his most charming smile and said, "What's up with that?"

Five

He really didn't think the question would be that hard for her to answer, nor could he believe it was one that came as any great surprise. Surely she'd heard it voiced in the past from at least a couple of people. Like, for instance, oh... Sean didn't know. Maybe from every single guy she'd ever dated? Judging by the look on her face when he posed the query, however, the topic was one that Autumn really didn't like to talk about. Because she offered not a single word in response.

"Autumn?" he said softly, thinking maybe she hadn't been paying attention or had misunderstood somehow.

She continued to gaze at him in silence for a moment, then shook her head once, as if to clear it. But all she managed by way of a response was, "Um."

"Yes?" he tried again.

This time she only said, "Well."

Sean tried another tack. "This can't be a new question

for you,'' he said, stating aloud his earlier thoughts. ''Can it?''

''Not…not really,'' she said, with considerably more eloquence this time. But she still didn't elaborate.

So Sean waited patiently, helping himself to another handful of popcorn, tipping back his wine to wash it down. He really wasn't accustomed to sacrificing one of his better bottles for the accompaniment of drive-in fare. But this was something of a special occasion, and Autumn was more than worth it.

And besides, the '83 Rothschild really did just go so nicely with popcorn.

When he heard a soft sigh emanate from the seat beside him, Sean pulled his attention back to the matter at hand.

''I suppose you do deserve an explanation,'' she said softly, twirling her own glass slowly by its stem.

''Well, you have to admit that it is something of an unconventional rule,'' he pointed out.

She nodded with clear reluctance. ''It's odd, you mean.''

''Free spirited,'' he corrected her.

She sighed heavily again, sipped her wine once more, then told him, ''To put it simply, Sean, the reason I never date a man for more than one lunar month is because I just can't trust myself around men.''

Funny, he thought, but she made that sound like a *bad* thing.

''What do you mean?'' he asked. Perhaps they were on two different wavelengths here, he thought.

She shrugged slightly, then lifted her wine to her lips for another idle sip. ''Just…I don't have very good judgment when it comes to men. I tend to get overly involved with…well, I might as well just say it…losers.''

Oh, they most definitely were *not* on the same wavelength, Sean thought.

Before he could comment, she glanced up at him again,

and when she saw the expression on his face, she hastily added, "Present company excluded, of course."

"Thanks," he answered dryly.

She dropped her gaze back to her wineglass. "I've just had a couple of bad experiences with men," she went on softly. "And I'd rather not repeat them."

Oh, was *that* all? Sean thought. "Yeah, well, no offense, Autumn, but anyone who's single has had some bad experiences with the opposite sex."

She shook her head slowly and avoided his gaze. "Not like mine," she vowed.

Sean chuckled with profound understatement. "Wanna bet?"

She snapped her head up at that, but only studied him in silence for a moment, as if she weren't sure what to say. Finally, quietly, she asked, "Have you ever been engaged?"

"No," Sean told her easily, immediately. "Never even came close."

"Well, I have," she said quietly.

He took some comfort in the fact that she didn't seem to be all that happy about having once made such a commitment. But a not-so-little part of him was surprisingly bothered by the fact that Autumn had, at some point in her life, loved another man enough to want to bind herself to him for all eternity.

Then it occurred to Sean how he had phrased that realization, and he frowned. *Another* man? Why would he think in such terms, he wondered? Why not just *a* man? *Another* man suggested that he considered Autumn's former fiancé to be a rival. And *rival* suggested that he wanted there to be something more substantial to what was happening between him and Autumn right now than there actually was. So how could her ex-fiancé be a rival when Sean was a two-lunar-month kind of guy?

And why did he suddenly have such a pounding headache?

He opened his mouth to comment on her revelation, but Autumn pressed on before he had the chance. "My first fiancé—"

"Whoa, whoa, whoa," Sean interrupted before he could stop himself. "Your *first* fiancé?"

She gazed steadily out the windshield, her face completely devoid of any expression. She did seem to be a bit pale, though, he noted. And he wasn't positive, but he thought she was speaking through gritted teeth when she replied shortly, "Yes. My first."

"Um, excuse me for prying," he said cautiously, "but just how many fiancés have you had?"

Still staring out into the darkness instead of at his face, she held up her hand, index and middle fingers extended. Sharply. Again, her words sounded strained when they came out. "Just two."

"*Just* two?" he repeated before he could stop himself.

Even in the darkness he could see her cheeks color with her embarrassment. "As I was saying," she began again meaningfully, "my first fiancé declined to show up at the church on our wedding day because he was out of town."

"Out of town?" Sean echoed. "On his own wedding day?"

She nodded stiffly.

"Um, where did he go?"

"To Puerto Vallarta."

"Oh." Then, hoping to salvage something of the news, he added, "Well, you know, I've heard Puerto Vallarta is really nice, and—"

"He went with a lap dancer named Rhonda," Autumn concluded crisply.

"Oh."

"And he used the plane tickets and hotel reservation that were supposed to be for our honeymoon."

"Oh."

"My second fiancé," she continued, her voice still way too starched and pressed, "missed our wedding because he was…otherwise detained."

Sean studied her thoughtfully for a moment. "Otherwise detained?"

"Yes."

When she didn't elaborate, he asked—very, *very* cautiously this time. "You mean he, like…got held up at work?"

"No."

"Um, traffic jam?"

"No."

"Hit by a bus?"

"No. Not a bus. He got hit with an arrest warrant."

Telling himself not to do it, but feeling the same morbid curiosity one experiences when passing a car accident, Sean somehow heard himself ask, "Um, what was he arrested for?"

Autumn inhaled a deep breath and released it slowly. "Bigamy," she told him.

"Oh."

"Actually, it was trigamy—he had three wives when he proposed to me."

"Oh."

"But I don't suppose trigamy is really a word, is it?"

"I suppose not."

"So, anyway," she pressed on valiantly, still gazing out the windshield instead of at Sean, "you can see why it's essential that I avoid getting too involved with anyone."

Actually, Sean couldn't see that at all. But something in her posture kept him from saying that. "And you think this lunar-month thing is the way to go about ensuring that?"

"It's as good a way as any," she said, her voice sounding as imperious as a queen's.

"You never date a guy for more than four weeks?" Sean asked, not sure why he was feeling so adamant about this.

"Never," she told him.

"No matter what?"

"No matter what."

He chewed his lower lip as he thought. "I can see why that would work well if you find yourself dating someone who doesn't, shall we say, toast your melbas."

That, finally, made her turn and look at him. Okay, turn and squint at him in total befuddlement, Sean amended, but at least he had her attention.

"But what if," he continued hastily, "at the end of the four weeks, you really like the guy you're dating?"

"I break up with him anyway."

Sean's eyebrows shot right up to his hairline. "You break up with him even if you like him?"

She nodded. "It's better than the alternative."

"What alternative? Dating him longer than four weeks?"

"Yes."

"Why is that better?"

"Because there's no risk that I'll grow to love him and want to marry him and then have him abandon me."

Sean bit back an unusually ripe expletive. "But what would happen if you *did* decide you wanted to see more of him?"

She shook her head slowly as she eyed him with much confusion. "That's never happened."

Again that odd surge of relief swept through him, but Sean didn't spare any time to contemplate it. "But what if it did?" he asked again.

"It won't."

"But what if it *did?*" he insisted.

She uttered a small sound of surprise and gaped softly

at him. "Well," she began slowly, thoughtfully, "I guess I'd have to break up with him, anyway."

"But why?" Sean asked, genuinely puzzled by her response.

She lifted her shoulders and let them drop uncomfortably. "Because I don't want to get hurt again."

"And you think you'll prevent that by never dating anyone longer than four weeks?"

"Yes."

"That's your *plan?*" he asked incredulously.

She reddened again, only this time it wasn't because she was embarrassed. This time it was because she was really, really angry. "Yes," she said coolly. "That's my plan. And it's a very good one."

"How do you figure?"

"Because it's worked very well."

"So far," he qualified.

"Oh, believe me, Mr. Monahan, it's still working, very, *very* well."

He opened his mouth to object again, realized she had just pretty much put him in his place, so opted not to make things any worse for himself than they already were. He could work this out, he told himself. He could.

He was, after all, Sean Monahan.

All in all, Autumn's second date with Sean Monahan didn't go nearly as well as the first. Where the first had been filled with awkward silences, stilted conversation, Don Knotts and popcorn that really had been just a tad too salty, the second was considerably more troubling. Because for that second date, Sean pulled up in front of Autumn's house in his older brother's Jaguar roadster, appeared at her front door dressed in an exquisitely tailored dark suit, and he took Autumn to Marigold's very finest restaurant, Bud Dooley's Tavern on the Stream.

Interestingly, the establishment wasn't actually on a
stream. It was, in fact, on a green. But Bud Dooley had
been concerned about being sued for trademark infringe-
ment, hence the alteration. The restaurant hadn't been rated
by the Michelin Guide, per se, but with just one look inside,
Autumn was confident the Tavern on the Stream would
have received at least three stars, and probably more like
three and a half.

Reminiscent of a Tudor alehouse—kind of—its furnishings were dark and elegant and, it rather went without saying, Elizabethan. Carpets patterned in dark, rich, jewel
tones spanned much of the dark hardwood floor, and the
walls repeated the vibrant—and likewise dark—colors.
Each room they passed was done in a different—and
dark—hue. The lights, too, were dimmed low, giving the
whole place an atmosphere that was, simply put, much too
romantic.

Ergo, much too troubling.

Autumn reminded herself that she could have easily
avoided this trouble. All she'd had to do was decline the
invitation Sean had extended when he'd brought her home
from the drive-in two nights ago. After all, she would have
had a good reason for declining, wouldn't she? That the
first date really hadn't gone particularly well, had it? So
why bother with a second?

In fact, she had intended to utter that very observation—
politely and tactfully, of course—once she'd unlocked her
front door after the drive-in, but when she'd turned back
around to do so, Sean had lifted a hand to cup it gently
beneath her jaw, and she'd been so surprised by the gesture
that she hadn't been able to speak. And then he'd leaned
forward without a word and kissed her good night—a brief,
chaste brush of his lips over her cheek and nothing more.
And then he'd murmured the softest ''Good night'' she'd

ever heard, in a voice that had set her heart to humming happily behind her ribs.

For one long moment, Autumn had only stared at him in stunned silence, having no idea what to say or do next. Well, actually that wasn't quite true. His kiss had given her a couple of ideas, but neither of them had been particularly acceptable. Not in mixed and polite company, at any rate. Certainly not in mixed and polite company who had made their acquaintance scarcely a week before. Once she got to know him better, of course, well *then* they could—

Well, then they could nothing, she told herself now, as she followed the hostess and preceded Sean into an especially beautiful, particularly dark, remarkably romantic dining room. She wasn't about to get to know Sean Monahan better. And even if she did get to know him better, she certainly wasn't going to get to know him like…like…well, like *that*.

Ruthlessly Autumn pushed that thought away, too, and tried to think about something else instead. Unfortunately, the thought that immediately erupted in her brain was of that good-night kiss two nights before. So, sighing in defeat, she let the thought unroll.

Despite the awkwardness of the evening at the drive-in, Sean had been a complete gentleman when he'd taken her home. She'd had a few dates who had considered the good-night ritual to be one where the man freely pawed and groped the woman, then stormed off in a huff when said woman shoved him away. And she'd had even more dates who had considered the good-night ritual to be one where the man came inside and chatted about his business, his history, his life and his expectations of a woman for an interminable length of time.

But Sean had only walked her to her front door and waited while she unlocked it, and he'd been tentative and solicitous when he'd brushed his lips softly over her cheek.

With one final, gentle, caress of his fingertips along her jawline, he'd asked very quietly, very courteously, if he could see her again on Friday. And Autumn had been helpless to do anything but say yes.

Then Sean had smiled, had told her he'd see her at six o'clock, and to wear something nice because he had a treat in store for her. She'd been too flummoxed to do anything but nod her silent agreement. Then he'd smiled again, her toes had curled, and that had been the end of that.

Now, of course, Autumn was having second thoughts, even if she had taken great care in selecting one of her nicer dresses—a sleeveless sheath of pale gold that fell in loose gauzy pleats to midcalf. And she found herself wishing that Sean had taken her somewhere other than Bud Dooley's. Like bowling, for example. She wasn't much of a bowler. Or to Cheezy Esther's House of Corn Dogs, another famous Marigold fixture. As popular as corn dogs were, Autumn had just never developed a taste for them herself. Had Sean taken her to one of those places, she'd be feeling awkward and uncomfortable again, and this time, Autumn was sure she'd be able to turn him down when—if—he asked her out again after taking her home.

But Bud Dooley's Tavern on the Stream was very much to her liking. And Sean Monahan in an exquisitely tailored dark suit was even more to her liking. She sneaked another glimpse at him over her shoulder as the hostess led them to their table, and somehow managed to bite back a sigh. He'd even gotten a haircut at some point over the past couple of days, she noted, and his razor-straight ebony hair caught the faint candlelight, tossing it back in sapphire flames. He had clearly just shaved—his jawline was fine and smooth, unmarred by shadow—and he smelled... Autumn inhaled deeply in spite of herself, sighing in delight as she exhaled. He smelled fresh and clean and masculine. The hostess smiled at Sean as she unfolded his leather-bound menu before him, and she also smiled at Sean as she unfolded Autumn's menu before her. The other woman— who, Autumn couldn't help but note, was tall and willowy and very, very blond—continued to smile at Sean as she placed the wine list on the table, and she smiled over her shoulder at Sean as she retreated to the hostess stand where, Autumn couldn't help noticing, she smiled at Sean some more.

"Friend of yours?" she asked idly as she scanned the pasta selections, telling herself she did *not* sound jealous.

"Hmm?" Sean asked absently, glancing up from his own menu. He gazed at her, faintly puzzled. "Is who a friend of mine?"

Autumn tipped her head to the side, reluctant to glance over at the hostess. Not just because it would be impolite, but because she was certain the woman was still smiling at Sean. "Blondie over there," she said before she could stop herself, wincing silently because this time she *knew* she sounded jealous—not to mention impolite. "Is she a friend of yours?"

Sean spared a brief glimpse at the hostess, then returned his attention to Autumn. As much as she tried to tell herself otherwise, he really didn't seem to have a single interest in the blonde. What he did seem to have an interest in was Autumn's response to the blonde.

"You mean Natasha?" he asked, the ghost of a smile playing about his—extremely attractive—mouth.

Natasha, she repeated to herself. Naturally the woman would have a name like that—sexy and exotic and mysterious. But all Autumn offered by way of a reply was a very mild "Mmm."

Sean's smile grew even more playful at her response. And oh, she really, really wished he wouldn't smile at her that way. Not so much because it was such a charming, irresistible smile, but because it was all too knowing. Dammit.

"Yeah, I know Natasha," he said. "We used to go to school together."

Still trying to pretend she wasn't at all interested, but knowing full well she was very close to making a fool of herself, Autumn asked, "Was that all you did together?"

"Nope."

Well, that certainly caught her attention. And also what little was left of her self-control. "What do you mean 'Nope'?" she demanded. Petulantly, too, dammit. Too late, she realized she had also slammed her menu down onto the table and was glaring at Sean as if she were his outraged lover.

And Sean had the nerve to chuckle at her reaction. *Dammit.* "She and I used to work together," he said, not even bothering to hide how very interesting he found her sudden interest.

Autumn relaxed a bit at hearing the obvious lack of wistfulness in his voice and seeing the obvious lack of regret in his expression. "Oh," she said with vast understatement. She picked up her menu and began to peruse it again.

"And, also, she used to be my girlfriend," Sean added blandly, returning his gaze to his own menu.

"What?" *Slam.* Down went the menu again.

"For a whole year," he said, fixing his interest on the lower right-hand side of his menu. "Hot and heavy our relationship was, too. Ooo, the beef medallions in burgundy looks good." He glanced up again, his expression now focused entirely on Autumn. "What looks good to you?"

What looked good to her, Autumn didn't want to talk about. "She was your girlfriend for a full year?" she asked, cursing herself for sounding so petulant. Cursing herself for *feeling* so petulant.

He seemed puzzled. "Who?"

"Her," she repeated.

"Her who?"

She expelled an exasperated sound and tipped her head to the side again. "Natasha," she whispered. At least, Autumn told herself she was whispering. She couldn't help it if it sounded more like hissing instead.

"Oh, her," Sean said with another one of those mild, toe-curling smiles. But still he offered no reply.

"Yes, her," Autumn spurred him. Now that she'd made a fool of herself, she wasn't about to let this go until she had all the answers she wanted.

But Sean frustrated her efforts once again. Because all he did was nod his answer to her question, then continue to gaze at her in that intent way of his. "So what looks good to you?" he repeated, as if the entire fate of the universe rested on her dinner choice.

"How long ago did you date her?" Autumn persisted.

"Who?"

"Natasha."

"Oh." He thought for a moment. "Let's see now…that would have been the summer after I got my first bike—a sapphire blue Stingray with a yellow banana seat—very cool. So that would have been…"

He began some quick mental tabulating, but Autumn's heart was already returning to its previous calm pulsing, before he told her, "When we were in second grade."

She narrowed her eyes at him, and when he started to smile that knowing little smile of his again, darned if her heart rate didn't skyrocket to the stratosphere once more. "You had a girlfriend when you were in second grade?" she asked, proud of herself for not hissing once. Somehow, though, she wasn't surprised by the information. Sean Monahan had probably had girls toddling after him from the moment he took his first step.

He nodded. "Hot and heavy," he reminded her. "Natasha always shared her graham crackers and marshmallow cream with me at snack time. And I, in turn, allowed her the honor of carrying my books home for me.''

Autumn studied him in silence for a moment more, then, ''I see,'' she said quietly.

''Hey, it was a big step in our relationship,'' he told her. ''Most guys would be too embarrassed to let a girl carry their books for them.'' He grinned with what was clearly proud satisfaction. ''But not me. I was comfortable in my masculinity. Even in second grade. That's why the girls always liked me so much.''

Autumn shook her head in bemusement, having no idea what to say to that. And she cursed herself one more time for having revealed to him just how much he was getting to her, for letting him know just how much she cared about his past, for giving him the impression that she thought there might just be some potential in this—

No. She would not call it a *relationship*. Two dates did not a relationship make, in any way, shape or form. What she and Sean had was... Hmm. Well, she wasn't exactly sure what they had. She supposed what the two of them had was...was... Well, it was two dates, that was all. Okay, two dates, and a mildly suggestive conversation about fireworks under a star-spangled sky. And also a shared bottle of good wine in the twilit darkness. And a nice—a really, really nice—good-night kiss on the cheek.

But that was it.

''So,'' Sean said for a third time, ''what looks good to you?''

This time when he said it, though, there was something different about the question. This time, he seemed to be talking about a lot more than food.

Autumn swallowed with some difficulty and dropped her gaze back to her menu. ''Actually,'' she finally said, ''I haven't had a chance to look yet.''

His voice was velvety smooth when he replied, "Well, then, by all means, Autumn, look. Look to your heart's content."

Oh, she didn't think that would be a good idea at all. Not because of the way his request wrapped itself so warmly around her and put ideas—oh, my...*such* ideas—into her head. But also because the last thing she needed was to be looking at Sean when she felt such an indolent, liquid heat meandering through her body, pooling in places that had no business feeling hot right now. Looking at him when she was feeling such things would no doubt reveal to him that she was, in fact, feeling such things. Unfortunately, the soft timbre of his voice, so obviously intended for her ears alone, was too delicious for her to ignore.

Carefully she lifted her gaze again, and she found Sean studying her with unmistakable—and uninhibited—desire. And with something else, too, something she couldn't help but notice, something that was almost wistful, almost sweet. And that wistful sweetness, even more than the uninhibited desire, twisted something inside her that was every bit as poignant. It was also, she couldn't help but admit, very confusing.

"Sean, I—"

Whatever Autumn had intended to say—and that was as big a mystery to her as it was to anyone—was prevented by the arrival of their server. And just like that, whatever had been going on inside Sean completely evaporated. Because he immediately schooled his features back into that vaguely amused expression that revealed nothing more than his good humor.

"My, um, my companion," he told the waiter, "is still looking. So you'll have to give us a few more minutes."

At least a few more minutes, Autumn thought. Because

she wasn't sure she'd *ever* get tired of looking at Sean Monahan.

She sighed again, this time in defeat. It was going to be an interesting night.

Six

As Sean strode around the front of his brother's Jag to open the passenger side door for his date, two thoughts were warring for possession of his brain. The first was that Finn really did know how to pick cars. The black Jag roadster was sleek and elegant and graceful, and it handled, oh... Just so beautifully. And the second thought was that Autumn Pulaski was an exceptionally attractive woman. Talk about sleek and elegant and graceful, he thought, never mind how beautifully she—

Well. He didn't really know about that part, did he? Not yet. Because he hadn't had the opportunity to, well, handle her, had he? Not yet. Nevertheless, judging by some of the come-hither looks he'd caught her throwing his way during dinner, that handling business just might not be too far off in the future. Certainly long before the completion of a lunar month.

He could hardly wait.

After opening the passenger side door, he extended a hand to help Autumn out of the car, inhaling deeply—but unobtrusively—as she rose. She smelled incredible. Not like freshly baked bread and cinnamon rolls this time, but of something spicy and earthy and exotic.

She looked exotic, too, he thought, unable to keep his gaze from roving all over her, even though he'd already inspected every last inch of her this evening, every time she hadn't been looking. And quite nice inches they were, too. At least, he thought further, backpedaling, he *hoped* she hadn't been looking when he'd made his earlier inspection. Of course, if she *had* been looking, she would have seen what he was sure must have been blazing in his eyes as he looked. And if she'd seen that, she would probably have run screaming in terror—or, at the very least, screaming in fear for her virtue—for the hills.

Sean pushed the thought away and went back to drinking his visual fill of her, even though he knew that particular thirst would probably never be satisfied. She had wound her hair up into some sort of elaborate twist that hugged the back of her head, and it appeared to be held in place by nothing more than a pair of large, gold-tipped, ivory-colored picks of some kind. Sean got the impression that with a couple of swift, deft maneuvers, he could pull the twin implements free and loose what he suspected was a thick, wild mane of burnt copper. He'd seen for himself that her hair, when braided, fell to nearly her waist, and he could just imagine what it would feel like to sift those long, silky tresses between his fingers.

Boy, could he imagine.

In fact, he could also imagine what it would feel like to have those long, silky tresses streaming over his bare chest as Autumn—likewise bare—straddled his lower body. And he could imagine—too well—what it would feel like to have the pressure of her naked thighs closing around his waist and hips, and what it would feel like when she kissed him long and hard and deep, and what it would feel like when she lowered herself over him to sheathe him snugly inside her—

Well. He was probably getting a little ahead of himself, there.

"Would you like to come in for coffee, Sean?"

Then again…

When his eyes met hers, though, he saw that Autumn seemed to be as surprised by the offer as he was. Not that Sean had said or done anything in particular this evening that might make her want to escape his company, but she hadn't exactly seemed eager to prolong the evening, either. Which was odd, because of those previously mentioned come-hither looks. And he still wasn't quite sure what to make of her reaction to Natasha. There had been a few moments, there, when Autumn had actually sounded like a jealous lover. That had to be good, right? Unless, of course, there was some kind of *Fatal Attraction* thing going on here.

Nah. No chance of that. Sean was certain it was his own irresistible appeal, and not a chemical imbalance in her brain, that was responsible for her reaction.

"I'd love to come in for coffee," he replied, before she had a chance to reconsider, which she was clearly tempted to do.

He couldn't tell if she was pleased by his acceptance or not, but she gave him a halfhearted little smile that was— Well, the word *enchanting* came to mind, even though that wasn't a word Sean would normally have admitted to being acquainted with.

But Autumn really was enchanting. There was an almost otherworldly quality about her, something that made her seem different from the average person. He wasn't sure if that was because of her unusual upbringing—though there was something of the wood sprite about her, he had to admit—or if it was just some innate quality that was uniquely hers. Whatever it was, though, it was damned nice, and it made Sean follow her to the front door like a puppy starved for the merest scrap of attention.

They made small talk as they strode up the cobbled walkway and wooden steps, then partook of chitchat while Autumn unlocked the front door. Sean hadn't bothered to take a look at his surroundings the other night when he'd brought her home—hey, why would he, when he'd had Autumn to look at instead?—but he took a moment to do so now. The house was small but tidy, a frame cottage painted barn-red with white trim. A vast assortment of colorful foliage spilled from bushes and baskets along the slatted porch, sprouted from the ground along the walkway and burst from boxes in each of the front windows.

He wasn't surprised to discover that Autumn liked to grow things. He was even less surprised to discover that she was good at it.

The inside of her house continued with the cozy-cottage theme, flowered hooked rugs spanning hardwood floors, chairs and sofa covered in a huge-cabbage-rose chintz, spindly little antique tables overflowing with...stuff. Extremely dainty, impossibly feminine...stuff. Lacy doilies, cut-crystal vases filled with flowers, sterling picture frames, potpourri. The mantelpiece played host to more stuff—silver candlesticks, bisque figurines and what appeared to be a scaled-down version of a grandfather clock.

And as much as Sean told himself he should loathe the decor, as adamantly as he assured himself that no self-respecting testosterone-producing unit would ever be comfortable in such a place—he tossed off a mental shrug—he liked it. He liked Autumn's place a lot. Probably because it reminded him very much of Autumn herself.

He was just thinking about how surprising it was that

she didn't have any cats to complement the cottage look—
and, of course, the I'll-never-date-anyone-longer-than-a-
lunar-month look—when he glanced up to find a large gray
monster wandering down the hall right toward him. And
although the creature did indeed appear to be feline in nature, it also looked perturbed enough to be a human. A very
grumpy human, at that.

"Oh, that's Moonshadow," Autumn said when she noted
where Sean's attention had strayed.

"Of course it is," he replied, smiling at the utter incon-
gruity of the moniker. Incongruous in terms of the cat, at
least—it was much too sweet a name for an animal who
obviously had a rather sour disposition. As a choice made
by Autumn Pulaski, however, the name came as no surprise
at all.

"He has two sisters, as well," she added, "Winterbourne
and Marmalade. But they're a bit shy. I doubt they'll make
an appearance."

As if they wanted to make a liar out of her—which, Sean
was certain, they did, because that was the way cats were,
after all—two more felines joined the first, one as white as
new-fallen snow, the other the color of, well, orange marmalade. Autumn had managed to give her cats names that
were both utterly predictable and wildly imaginative. Why
was he not surprised?

"I'll just get the coffee started," she added, sounding a
bit breathless for some reason.

Sean returned his attention to Autumn, to see why she
might be feeling breathless, but she'd turned her back on
him and was quickly making her way down the hall. The
squeakity-squeakity-squeaksqueaksqueak of old wooden
floor punctuated her escape, and something about the sound
made his smile crook higher.

He took his time following her, noting the watercolor
prints that hung on the hallway walls, and how each of the

rooms he passed continued with the English countryside theme. One room was clearly a home office, filled to capacity with all manner of clutter, but somehow even the clutter looked charming. The other room was Autumn's bedroom, he realized, and his heart rate jacked higher as he noted the lushness of the furnishings. He didn't dare stop to gaze openly into the room, because Autumn might have misinterpreted his interest. Or, worse, she would have *correctly* interpreted his interest. And then she would have thrown him out on his keester, because his interest was licentious in the extreme.

But in that single leisurely pass, Sean noted quite a bit about Autumn's private, intimate domain. He noticed it was, again, ultrafeminine, an ivory crocheted coverlet and canopy spanning a *very* comfortable-looking full-size, four-poster bed. Which was kind of strange, because normally, a full-size bed would seem much too small to be comfortable. However, when Sean took into account that anyone sleeping—or whatever—in this particular bed would also be sleeping—or whatever—with Autumn, it somehow seemed the perfect size.

Adding to the relaxing—or whatever—mood, a veritable mountain of throw pillows, all in soft, barely-there colors, was piled at the head, and a fuzzy-looking throw was tossed across the foot. A dark-brown wicker rocking chair—almost certainly antique—beckoned from the corner. And a matching wicker chest—almost certainly filled with womanly whatnots—played host to a grouping of plants beneath a lace-covered window. The wallpaper was old-fashioned tiny pink flowers against a yellow background, and the accent pieces were all throwbacks to another, simpler time.

And all Sean could think as he completed his survey was that there was something inexplicably erotic about the prospect of making love, specifically to Autumn, amid such surroundings. Something about her very feminine world just made him feel that much more masculine, and his desire—nay, his intent—to make love to her, in that very bed, multiplied ten times over.

"It shouldn't be long," he heard her say from the kitchen.

No, it shouldn't, he thought to himself as he turned around to complete his journey.

"The coffee, I mean," she clarified as he entered the kitchen, as if she feared he might be misinterpreting her remark and thinking she meant something else. Something like, oh, say…exactly what he had been thinking about.

"Mmm," he said noncommittally. But he offered nothing more that might reveal the avenue his own thoughts had taken.

"Would you like dessert?" she asked, sounding every bit as nervous as she looked like she felt. "We overdid the éclairs today at the bakery, so I sent some home with everyone, and brought a couple for myself. We didn't have dessert at the restaurant," she added unnecessarily.

No, they hadn't had dessert, Sean recalled. Autumn hadn't asked, and he hadn't suggested. Not just because he'd been full by then, but because he'd rather hoped to have dessert here. Of course, his idea of dessert and Autumn's idea of dessert were no doubt wildly at odds. She was thinking along the lines of sweet, delicate pastries, while he was thinking along the lines of, well, hot monkey love. Although when he thought about the introduction of éclairs now…

Nah. No sense getting chocolate all over those beautiful sheets.

"I'd love dessert," he told her.

Autumn smiled—nervously.

Sean smiled back—triumphantly.

Oh, this was going to be so-o-o-o easy. He wondered if she had any extra whipped cream….

* * *

Autumn wasn't sure she liked the way Sean was looking at her when she glanced up to find him looking at her. Well, she *liked* the way he was looking at her. She just wasn't sure she liked the way she *felt* when she saw him looking at her the way he was looking at her. Actually, that wasn't true, either. She *did* like the way she felt when she saw him looking at her the way he was looking at her. But she was pretty sure she *shouldn't* be liking the way she felt when she saw him looking at her the way he was looking at her. Not with him looking at her the way he was looking at her, anyway.

Or something like that. Suddenly, for some reason she felt so confused…

And dizzy. Why did she feel so dizzy? And why was she so warm? Was it warm in here? It was definitely much too warm in here.

With a quick—but hopefully imperceptible—shake of her head, Autumn returned her attention to the matter at hand…even if she couldn't quite remember what that matter was exactly. All she could do was keep a cautious eye on Sean, and marvel at how the way he was looking at her now was so much different from the way he had been looking at her earlier in the evening.

Ooooh, yeah. Now she remembered what the matter at hand was.

And all over again she began to grow hot and dizzy and confused. Because although some of Sean's earlier looks had been pretty warm, the ones he was sending her way now were downright incandescent. Something had changed between them over the course of the evening, and Autumn couldn't quite say when it had happened or even what it was. Everything had seemed to be moving along nicely at the restaurant—once she'd gotten past that Natasha business, anyway. But now that they were here in her house, where she should have felt very comfortable...

Well, Autumn felt anything *but* comfortable.

What she felt was agitated. Anxious. Expectant. And, of course, hot. Really hot. Somehow it seemed as if there was something very important she needed to do, but she couldn't quite think what it was. And there stood Sean, gazing at her as if he wanted to make *her* dessert, instead of the éclairs, and—

It finally hit her then, like a ton of pastry dough, just what was going on. He *did* want to make her dessert instead of the éclairs. That was why he was looking at her the way he was looking at her. That was why she felt the way she was feeling. And that was why she liked that feeling *so much.*

Uh-oh.

It was happening again. Autumn was falling fast for a handsome, charming, eligible man. *Oh, no...* She bit back a growl of frustration. This couldn't possibly be happening. Not now. Not yet. They hadn't even made it through the first week of the lunar month. It wasn't fair.

This was terrible!

She liked Sean. She didn't want to have to break up with him already. She'd been hoping to get at least three weeks in with him before she started succumbing to his handsome, charming eligibility. She'd been so sure she was mature enough to withstand his obvious allure. She'd been so positive that she had enough experience with men by now that Sean would only be one more in a string of lunar-month success stories. Yes, he was infinitely more appealing than any of the other men she'd met in Marigold. But she'd thought she had enough willpower to last longer than *this.*

She sighed heavily. Damn. She was going to have to put an end to things now. Tonight. As soon as they finished their coffee and éclairs, she would have to send Sean packing. And she'd have to come up with some kind of acceptable excuse between now and then for why she was breaking it off, because they'd had a surprisingly good time tonight. He wasn't going to buy it if she told him they just weren't compatible, because she suspected that, with time, the two of them might be very compatible indeed—which, of course, was part of the problem, but somehow, she didn't think he'd understand that part. And he certainly wasn't going to believe her if she told him she just didn't feel comfortable around him, because their date tonight had been nothing like the awkward one that had preceded it.

Once they'd gotten past that Natasha business, at any rate.

Because tonight they'd had a very nice conversation over dinner, about their work, their backgrounds, their education, their hopes, their dreams... And so often the two of them had just clicked right into place. Even when they'd held different opinions or offered different observations, those opinions and observations had somehow complemented each other. It was almost as if the two of them had been made for each other. Which, of course, wasn't possible. Autumn, for all her mystical and spiritual awareness, didn't believe in fate. Oh, she may have believed in it once upon a time, but those days were lo-o-o-o-ong gone.

Still, Sean did feel like such a comfortable fit.

What to do, what to do...

"Sounds like the coffee's ready," he said, gesturing toward the state-of-the-art brewer that was perched on her countertop.

If nothing else, his comment offered her a short-term solution to her long-term problem. For now she tried to forget about ending the evening and focused on enjoying the moment instead. After all, there were still quite a few moments left between now and later, she reminded herself, so she might as well enjoy each and every one of them.

After all, what could Sean possibly say or do in a matter of moments—however many they managed to eke out— that might change her mind about ending their... their...their liaison? Yes, that word would do nicely. It wasn't as if he was likely to change her mind. In her lunar-month rule, if in nothing else, Autumn had very strong convictions.

With a brief smile for Sean, she moved across the kitchen, then took her time preparing their dessert. She arranged a pair of éclairs on two rose-patterned dessert plates, then nestled two porcelain cups into matching saucers and filled each with dark, fragrant coffee. Then, without asking Sean his preferences, she withdrew the sugar bowl from the cupboard and filled the creamer with cream, because that was the way she liked her coffee—and also to buy herself a few more of those precious moments and to keep herself from having to look up and see him looking at her *that* way again.

By the time she'd completed her preparations and placed everything just so on a tray to carry their dessert and coffee to the living room, the silence between the two of them had begun to grow taut—and Autumn's skin had begun to grow hot. She was all too aware of Sean watching every move she made from the doorway, and even more aware of the heat shimmying up and down her spine under his steady perusal.

Oh, yes. She would definitely have to put an end to this tonight. Just having him in the same room was threatening to make her spontaneously combust. Among other things.

"Can I do anything to help?" he asked, finally removing himself from his leisurely stance to stride even more leisurely—and intentionally—toward her. This in spite of the fact that she was moving toward him, clearly with the intention of leaving the kitchen entirely.

Oh, yes, Autumn thought as she drew nearer. *You can*

stop being so handsome, so charming and so eligible. That
would help enormously.

Out loud, though, she only said, "I think I have it."

"You certainly do."

She glanced up in surprise at the tone of his voice—a
very dark, very sultry, very seductive tone of voice. And
when she saw the look in his eyes—a very dark, very sultry,
very seductive look—she felt the tray of coffee supplies
begin to slip from her suddenly numb fingers. And, feeling
helpless to halt the disaster—her fingers weren't the only
thing that went numb—Autumn could only watch with a
kind of disembodied fascination as the tray began to tip
dangerously forward.

It was only Sean's swift intervention that diverted certain
catastrophe. Quickly, smoothly, he intercepted the dipping
tray, sweeping it out of Autumn's possession to set it grace-
fully on the kitchen table, with nary a drop of coffee spilled.
And again she watched the motion with a detached kind of
interest, feeling as if she were someone else entirely, and
that what was happening there in her own kitchen couldn't
possibly be happening to her. Then Sean glanced up, and
she saw that look in his eyes again, and she suddenly realized how close he was—close enough that she could
smell the faint traces of his cologne, could see flecks of
midnight in his otherwise pale-blue eyes, could sense the
heat that surrounded him...surrounded her...surrounded
them.

And then, before she realized what was happening, he
was leaning forward, and then suddenly—and she had no
idea how it happened, truly—he was covering her mouth
with his. It was quite an extraordinary kiss. But then, he
was quite an extraordinary man. Oh, yes. Quite extraordinary indeed....

He started off slowly and tentatively, with just a whisper-
soft brush of his lips over hers, once...twice...three

times…four—oh, Autumn hoped it would never, ever end—then gradually built to something that was… *Oh, my.* Much less slow and much less tentative. Oh, yes, he definitely knew what he was doing now…. So what else could she do but go along for the ride?

And what a ride it was.

As if from a very great distance, Autumn registered a soft murmur of sound and was surprised to realize she was the one who had uttered it. But she couldn't help herself. The sensation of his fingertips skimming along the bare skin of her arms was just too delicious to ignore. Up and down, up…and…down, slower, then faster, then slow once again. His touch never strayed farther than her wrists or her shoulders, but he continued with that maddeningly erratic pace that mimicked the subtle, irregular motion of his mouth brushing over hers.

Before she even realized she had planned to do it, Autumn took a single step forward, an action that brought her body nearly flush against his. And then, without thinking, she lifted her hands to his chest, splaying them wide, pushing them higher, until she could curve her fingers possessively over the broad, strong line of his shoulders. The fabric of his jacket was cool and smooth—such a contrast to what she suspected was hot, tempered steel beneath.

And this time the soft sound that went up around them was a growl of masculine intent, because her touch was, evidently, all the encouragement Sean needed. The moment she made that voluntary physical contact, he deepened his kiss, looping one arm around her waist to pull her closer still, lifting his other hand to drag his fingers gently along the sensitive column of her throat. Autumn responded in kind, cupping her hand over his warm nape, then knifed the fingers of her other through his dark, silky hair. Then she tipped her head to the side so that she might, oh…take control of the kiss herself for a bit.

Surprisingly Sean demurred to her silent request, parting his lips fractionally in invitation for her to explore at will. Instinctively she trailed the tip of her tongue over the plump fullness of his lower lip, smiling at his gasp of surprise, opening her palm over the back of his head to cradle him in her hand. Then, feeling dangerous and wicked, she traced the upper contours of his mouth, as well, before dipping subtly inside for a more intimate taste of him. And oh, how delicious he tasted. Suddenly Autumn felt ravenous again, and somehow she knew that éclairs and coffee just weren't going to be enough to assuage this particular hunger.

She sensed that Sean felt that way, too, because he tilted his head to the other side then and seized control of the kiss once again. And as he plundered her mouth more resolutely, as he kissed her and kissed her and kissed her some more, he reached up and, in one smooth, quick gesture, freed the two picks that had kept her French twist in place. Immediately her hair cascaded over her shoulders and back, down to her waist. Without missing a beat, Sean filled both greedy hands with the silky tresses and kissed her more deeply still.

She wasn't sure how long they remained entwined that way, perhaps seconds, perhaps centuries, but he never once released her hair, no matter where he let his hands stray. And oh, how he let them stray. Up and down her back, over her shoulders, along her neck and jaw and throat. And once, when Autumn tipped her head backward, she felt a gentle tug on her hair as he cupped both hands possessively over her derriere, to pull her insistently into the cradle of his thighs, against the long, hard length of him. The sensation that shot through her at that intimate contact was exquisite, and she cried out almost ferally, so intense was her response.

Sean responded in kind, swallowing her outcry before it was complete, then dragging his mouth lower, along her jaw and neck and the sensitive hollow at the base of her throat. His breathing grew more ragged when he dipped his head lower still, running the tip of his tongue along her collarbone and breastbone, nuzzling the entrance to the dusky valley between her breasts. And when his movements grew even less focused and even more frantic, it was all Autumn could do to stay vertical. Her knees were weak, her entire body was limp, and if she wasn't careful, she was going to—

Oh, no. She already *was*. She was already more than halfway gone, *this close* to surrendering completely to what Sean clearly wanted to do. To what *she* clearly wanted to do. To what *they* clearly were about *to* do!

Atomic wind could not have moved faster than Autumn did in that moment. One minute she was erotically entwined with Sean, preparing to plunder him at will, and the next, she was standing on the other side of the kitchen table, gripping its edge to keep herself standing, gasping for breath to keep herself from fainting and groping for coherent thought to help her figure out why on earth she had just done what she had done.

This was only going to make breaking up with him even harder.

When she finally, finally managed to brave a glimpse at Sean, she found that he was no more under control than she was. His dark hair was in a state of total disarray, as if some woman half-gone on him had raked her hands through it over and over and over again. His necktie was completely undone, hanging unfettered from his collar, and although Autumn couldn't remember freeing it herself, she recalled that Sean's hands had been busy—very busy— elsewhere, therefore she must have been responsible for that particular development, which was pretty amazing, because that had been a Windsor knot. And his eyes...

Oh, my.

His eyes were fairly ablaze with a need and a wanting that she feared only mirrored her own.

Her first instinct was to release the table and rush right back into his arms, to throw caution to the wind and wrestle him to the floor, where she could have her way with him. Repeatedly. So naturally, what she did was say, "That shouldn't have happened."

He continued to gaze at her with undisguised—and very rampant—hunger as he replied, "Funny you should say that. Because something tells me that not only should it definitely have happened, but that it was completely unavoidable. And," he added meaningfully, "something tells me that it's going to happen again. Soon."

Autumn shook her head. "No, I don't think so." Somehow, though, the words came out completely lacking in conviction.

One corner of his mouth crooked into something of a grin. "Don't you?"

She shook her head again, but this time no words emerged at all.

He inhaled a deep breath and released it slowly, and Autumn couldn't help but note how shaky his respiration was. Without a word, and without once breaking eye contact, he made his way slowly around the table toward where she stood. Autumn told herself to run, to flee, to hie herself hence, to get herself to a nunnery or a cannery or a traveling carnival, anything...but Sean's steady gaze had her pinned to the spot.

He halted when a good six inches still lay between them, but she couldn't decide whether she was relieved or not. Then he lifted a hand to her hair once more, twined a solitary strand around and around and around his index finger. Then he bent forward slightly and brushed his lips over her cheek, a brief, chaste kiss that was totally at odds with the fervent embrace they had just shared.

And then he stepped away, releasing her hair as he went, and said, very softly, "I have to go."

Autumn swallowed with some difficulty, but for the life of her all she could think to say was, "But...but...we never had dessert."

He smiled, a sexy little smile that set her heart kathumping like a jackhammer in her chest. "Oh, yes, we did," he replied, just as softly. "It just wasn't quite as...satisfying as it will be next time." Then he spun on his heel and strode out of her kitchen.

And when she heard the creak of the front door and the quiet snick of the latch as it closed behind him, all Autumn could think was, *Next time? But there wasn't supposed to be any next time.*

And only then did she realize that she'd forgotten all about breaking it off with Sean before things could get out of hand.

Seven

As Sean took his time awaking the morning following his second, and much more successful, date with Autumn Pulaski, he could almost convince himself that he'd dreamed that exploratory little interlude in her kitchen the night before. Almost. It wasn't hard to do, after all, because he'd had quite a few similar dreams since stumbling into her bakery that fateful morning… Man. Had it only been a week ago? Dreams where the two of them were fairly wrapped around each other, usually naked, in settings as varied as a sun-splashed beach and, well, dangling from a ski lift. He'd rather liked that one.

But now as he gradually awoke and launched himself into a full-body stretch, he recalled with a fond smile that their embrace the night before—though it hadn't quite measured up to the ski lift scenario—had been real. Very real. Very pleasantly real. Very pleasantly, erotically real.

He could hardly wait to see her again.

But he wouldn't be seeing her today.

No, Sean had a plan in mind, a plan in *place,* that would ensure that his one lunar month with Autumn segued smoothly into two, and that plan meant staying away from her today. He'd formulated the plan the very night Finn had challenged him to date Autumn for two lunar months, and he'd rehearsed it in his head so many times he had it completely memorized. And so far everything—every last detail—was going precisely according to schedule.

Well, except for that strange heat that had totally swamped him on their first meeting. That had kind of come out of left field and had been a development Sean hadn't anticipated at all. But, now that he thought about it, that had actually helped matters, instead of hindering them. Heat was good for his plan. And, hey, his plan was moving along perfectly so far.

Okay, except maybe for the double feature at the Skyway that night having been Disney instead of the *Coeds-in-Heat Marathon* he'd been so sure was running. But that was okay, too. Coeds in heat might have actually made things between him and Autumn move along *too* quickly, in which case maybe, just maybe, he might have misjudged on that little part of his plan. But in hindsight everything had worked out for the best, because that unexpected generation of heat at their initial meeting had created all the combustion either of them really needed to get things moving along. So having the Disney thing happen was, on second thought, not such a bad development.

So everything was going exactly according to his plan.

Except, maybe, for the way he'd nearly jumped *way* ahead of schedule last night and made love to Autumn weeks—or, at the very least, several days—before he'd originally had that slotted in his plan. They'd stopped themselves in time, hadn't they? Or at least Autumn had stopped them. Nothing had happened that couldn't be repaired. Everything was still moving along according to his agenda. His plan hadn't been thrown off at all. Well, not much. Not really.

It was a good plan. It was.

And other than those few things—and, okay, maybe a few other, very minor, things—everything was running along *exactly* according to that plan. And for today the plan stated very explicitly, "Stay away from Autumn."

It was especially important to keep his distance today, considering how last night had turned out. Because they really did need to slow things down some. As much fun as he'd had last night with Autumn, Sean knew better than to oversaturate her with his presence. Putting all modesty aside—which was always easy for him to do—no woman could handle him in frequent doses, no matter how small. And after last night's dose, well... He supposed he and Autumn both ought to be relieved that neither of them had OD'ed.

But, wow, what a way to go.

Sean smiled as he relaxed his stretch, then arced his hands above his head and loosely gripped the headboard. As he lay naked in his bed, staring at the ceiling, he replayed last night over in his head yet again. He'd never known anyone who felt as good to hold as Autumn Pulaski did. All softness and warmth and curves and woman. She'd filled his arms so perfectly, had been so sweet to hang on to. And that hair... Sean sighed heavily as he recalled the heavy silkiness sifting through his fingers, spilling over his hands, skimming the insides of his wrists.... Boy. A man could get lost in that hair, he thought, closing his eyes. And he'd probably never find his way back...

He let his thoughts drift to the sublime for a moment, then, when the images dancing in his head started to become much too graphic, he quickly reined them back in. When he opened his eyes, he was still lying naked in his bed, head cradled in both palms, staring up at the ceiling. And what he saw in his mind's eye was still Autumn, naked this time, save the dark auburn stream of her hair flowing over her soft, pink flesh.

Well, he thought, *maybe* it might not hurt to see her again today. Just for a little while. That wouldn't mess up his plan *too* much. He didn't want her to have to go cold turkey, after all. That would be cruel. And, hey, who said he couldn't alter his plan a bit from time to time if he wanted to? It was *his* plan.

And it was a good one, too.

Because it was Saturday, Sean knew Autumn would be working at the bakery. Although he'd only formally met *her* the weekend before, he was fairly familiar with her place of business, living right around the corner from Autumn's Harvest as he did. He didn't frequent the place himself—he was a bacon-and-eggs breakfast kind of guy—but he'd walked past the bakery often enough in the mornings to know she did a booming business that time of day, particularly on the weekends. He'd also heard that her blueberry-banana-nut bread and orange-cranberry muffins were especially prized among the breakfast set. Those who weren't carnivores, anyway.

Upon arriving at the bakery, Sean saw that today was no different from any other weekend morning at what Marigoldians had come to affectionately call "The Harvest." When he strode through the front door of the shop area— or, more correctly, shouldered his way through the crowd milling around the entrance—he could barely fit inside, because the place was virtually filled to capacity.

Keen eye that he was—now that he'd had his morning coffee—he noticed right off that everyone else was fiercely grasping a paper number. So he, too, stepped up to the counter—or, more correctly, fought his way through the crowd until he could just manage to just reach the little machine spitting out the numbers, then had to wrestle for the next ticket with a surly adolescent who cut in front of him at the last minute. Finally surrendering—because he was polite, and *not* because the kid was far more dexterous than he—Sean glanced down at the number he eventually *did* retrieve, then up at the number on the wall. And then he sighed heavily.

Because the number he held in his hand was sixty-eight, and the little electronic sign on the wall read, "Now serving number forty-seven." He was about to grumble something under his breath that was more than a little *im*polite, when he suddenly realized that, gee, he didn't mind waiting, after all. Because there, working the counter, was Autumn Pulaski herself.

She was dressed in her baker's togs of white peasant blouse, white apron, white skirt and white kerchief tied pirate-style on her head, her long, burnished braid hanging heavily over one shoulder. Her cheeks were flushed from the heat and activity, and something about that reminded Sean of last night, and he began to feel a little flushed—among other things—himself.

Although she was clearly hurried, her movements were graceful and deft, and she smiled as she worked the crowd. Little by little Sean managed to make his way closer to the part of the counter she was working, but she never once glanced up to notice him, not even when he stood almost directly across from her. Because he was number sixty-eight, and by that time the little electronic sign on the wall read, "Now serving number fifty-nine."

And number fifty-nine, Sean realized then, just so happened to be Chuck Nielssen, whom Sean had known since high school, and whom he'd always considered to be much too tall and much too blond and much, *much* too overdeveloped, but whom women had always seemed to find attractive in a Nordic-god kind of way, go figure.

Autumn, Sean soon realized, much to his irritation, was no less immune. Dammit. Because she hadn't even finished announcing the word *nine*—had, in fact, barely enunciated the first consonant—when her gaze met Chuck's, and Chuck's gaze met hers, and then Sean himself could almost hear the subtle strains of "Ohhh, sweet mystery of youth, at last I've fooouuund yooou" go swelling up symphonically. And it just so happened to keep perfect time with the zinging of the strings of her heart. Dammit.

And all he could think then was that it was a damned good thing he'd altered his plan—again—today and come looking for her. Because, although Autumn Pulaski might think she was very good at making rules of the lunar-month variety, she clearly didn't know the first thing about plans of the *good* variety.

Before Sean could open his mouth to point that out to her, though, Chuck shouldered his way in front of him, stepped up to the counter and cut off any further view Sean might have enjoyed of Autumn. Worse than that, though, Chuck had the temerity to greet her with a smile and a deeply uttered, very resonant, "Hello, Autumn."

Damn the man.

Although Sean couldn't see her, he could certainly hear her when she replied, and he decided very quickly that he didn't like her tone of voice, that sweet, dripping-with-honey tone she used when she returned the other man's greeting with a soft, musically lilting, "Why, hello, Chuck."

Damn the woman.

"What's special today?" Chuck further queried. "Other than you, I mean," he added with a none-too-subtle laugh.

Sean tried not to vomit. He also tried to forget that what

the other man had just uttered was a line he'd used himself a time or two, usually with very good results.

Dammit.

Autumn's response was a titter of laughter, followed by a quiet, playful, "Oh, Chuck. You do say the sweetest things."

Again, Sean tried not to vomit. He also tried to forget that the way Autumn had just responded to the other man was the same way many a woman had responded to Sean when he'd said what Chuck had just said, women who later fell right into his—

Dammit.

"Have I ever told you," Chuck went on, still talking to Autumn, but jerking Sean out of his reverie, "just how beautiful you are in white?"

"Oh, Chuck."

"And how nice it is that you always smell so cinnamony sweet?"

"Oh, Chuck."

"And how your blueberry-banana-nut bread is just about the most delicious thing I've ever put in my mouth?"

"Oh, Chuck."

"Oh, Chuck?" Sean couldn't help cutting in.

The other man, bigger, blonder and more Nordic-looking than ever, turned to glower down at Sean, clearly none too happy to be interrupted during this elaborate mating ritual that obviously required more brain power than the guy was used to generating.

Glowering *down* at him, Sean noted again. He recalled then that Chuck Nielssen, although a bit deficient in the light bulb department, was a good six inches taller than he, something that had made varsity football practice more than a little unpleasant at times.

"Monahan," Chuck greeted him coolly. "You got a problem?"

Sean shook his head and forced a bland smile. "Not at all. I was just wondering if you got that, um…" He lowered his voice a bit, but not enough so that Autumn wouldn't overhear. "That…little problem taken care of?"

Chuck narrowed his ice-blue eyes and arrowed his pale blond brows downward. "What little problem?"

"You know," Sean said meaningfully. "That little *problem.* That little problem that everyone in Marigold is talking about. I heard about it from the rumor mill myself, so it must be true."

But Chuck only shook his head, clearly mystified. Then again, Sean thought, why should his condition today be any different from his condition every other day? Mystification was pretty much Chuck Nielssen's natural state.

Sean feigned discomfort. "Gee, Chuck, maybe I shouldn't have brought it up here this way. But I was worried about you. I know that, usually, a little shot of penicillin clears it right up, but—" he shrugged magnanimously "—then again, what's a little gonorrhea among friends, right? Guess that's why they call it a *social* disease."

Chuck's mouth dropped open in very clear, very real outrage, and for a moment he said nothing. Then, "Gono—" he began. He didn't finish, though. Not because he couldn't pronounce the word—though Sean wouldn't have been surprised if that had something to do with his hesitation—but also because he grabbed a fistful of Sean's shirt just then and shoved him up against the pastry case. Hard.

"What the hell are you talking about?" Chuck demanded.

"Chuck, please!" Autumn cried, reaching across the glass counter to wrap both her hands around the man's big, beefy forearm.

Well, hell, Sean thought. He hadn't wanted her to react

by *touching* the guy. He'd wanted her to react by recoiling in horror from him. This wasn't working out at all.

But the minute Autumn's hands made contact with Chuck's arm, the other man immediately released Sean. Each man eyed the other with much resentment for a couple of silent, tension-filled moments, then Sean turned to look at Autumn. Instead of appearing fearful for his safety, however, she had fisted both hands on her hips—and quite nice hips they were, too, he couldn't help noting—and was glaring at him. Glaring! At him! When he was the one who'd just been victimized!

"Hey, don't get mad at me. I was the victim here," he reminded her.

She flattened her lips into a tight line. "Were you?"

He gaped at her. "How can you even ask that? Of course I was."

But instead of answering him, Autumn turned back to Chuck. "What can I get for you?" she asked in a voice that was the absolute picture of politeness.

Chuck leered at her for a moment, tossed Sean a triumphant smile, then leered at her some more. "I like your cookies," he said in a lascivious voice. Then he went on to list a few other of Autumn's specialties that he clearly wanted to sample. And Autumn, being the gracious businesswoman that she was, happily supplied him with each and every one. She even gave him an extra chocolate chip cookie because of what she termed his "unpleasant experience in my normally peaceful establishment."

Dammit.

By the time the little sign on the wall finally, finally said, "Now serving number sixty-eight," Sean had flat-out run out of patience, Autumn was looking more frazzled than he'd ever seen her look, and the surly little punk who'd cut in front of him had taken the last lemon bar, the one Sean had been eyeing ever since Chuck had shoved him up against the pastry case holding them.

Dammit.

"How can I help you?"

It wasn't Autumn who asked the question when Sean turned over his little paper number, but one of the teenagers who worked for her. He was about to tell the girl in no uncertain terms *exactly* what he wanted—from her employer, at any rate—then he reminded himself that the kid was a minor, and he could get into a whole lot of trouble for that.

So he only said halfheartedly, "I'll take a couple of those asiago-cheese bagels and a loaf of that seven-grain onion dill."

"You want those sliced?"

What Sean really wanted, this girl didn't need to know. It would only lead to reform school. For both of them. "Yeah, why not?" he muttered irritably.

But his gaze was on Autumn as he said it, and he couldn't help noticing that she had her back to him.

Dammit.

The last thing Autumn needed on a busy Saturday morning was to have Sean Monahan standing on the other side of the counter looking like…like… Oh, God. Like the way he always looked. Handsome. Charming. Eligible. Irresistible.

Dammit.

She did her best to focus entirely on working her way through the morning rush, but every time she glanced up from that work, she found herself searching the crowd for Sean and, worse, finding him. And every time her gaze met his, she saw something burning in his eyes that she really, really wished would go out. Unfortunately, every time her gaze met his, whatever it was that was burning there only leaped higher and burned hotter, raising her own body's temperature to very dangerous levels.

At this rate it was going to be a very long lunar month. And they still had three weeks to go. What on earth had she been *thinking?*

Her conviction that she'd made a terrible, terrible mistake in agreeing to date Sean Monahan was only reinforced—again—at around eleven-thirty, when she looked up to find that he was still hanging around the shop area, drinking what she guessed to be his fifth cup of coffee and consuming what had to be his fourth asiago-cheese bagel. Naturally, she knew the bagels were delicious, but even at that, Sean's enthusiasm seemed a tad unrealistic. Especially since the rest of her morning patrons had dwindled down to a few stragglers, and the shop was nearly empty but for him.

She inhaled a deep breath, knowing the lull in business wouldn't last. Shortly after lunchtime, The Harvest would be hit again, and she'd be right back to rushing around behind the counter with the rest of her staff. So, as was her habit during these down times, Autumn decided to retreat to her office to knock off a little paperwork and see to some other business matters.

She had just turned in that direction when she heard Sean summon her by name, and she was forced to pivot back around.

"Yes?" she asked, trying not to notice how handsome, how charming and how eligible he looked in his softly worn jeans and skin-tight black T-shirt.

Really it was much, much too tight, she thought of the garment, as evidenced by the way it hugged every lovely ripple in his lean, muscular torso. And his jeans were no better, molding so beautifully every solid rope of sinew in those strong thighs. Honestly. How could he go out in pub-

lic looking that way? she wondered. It was scandalous.
Didn't he even look in a mirror?

He ambled up to a place exactly opposite hers at the
counter, then smiled a seductive little smile. Oh, dear.

"There seems to be a break in the action," he pointed
out unnecessarily, nodding his head briefly back at the
nearly empty shop.

"Yes, this is pretty much standard for this time of day,"
she told him. "It will pick up after lunch."

"So then, you could take a little break?" he asked hopefully.

"Actually, I like to use these times to catch up on paperwork," she said reluctantly.

He frowned, tsking softly. "All work and no play, Autumn..." But he left the admonition incomplete. Not that
any completion was necessary.

She had no idea why she said it—she really did have a
lot of paperwork to catch up on—but she heard herself
reply, "All right. I guess a little break wouldn't hurt."

"Hey, you have to eat sometime," he reminded her with
another one of those libido-grabbing, heart-stopping smiles.

Only when he mentioned it did Autumn realize how hungry she was. Strangely, being surrounded by baked goods
all day often hindered her appetite, and she was usually so
busy she simply forgot to stop long enough to recharge.
But the mention of food now made her mouth water. Or
maybe that was happening because of Sean's tight clothing.
Of course, Sean's tight clothing might also have been responsible for why she was so hungry....

"Something to, um, eat, sounds good," she told him
pertly, nudging her errant thoughts away.

Which was how Autumn came to be sharing her desk
with Sean Monahan over lunch. Well, as much of her desk
as she could share, seeing as how it was pretty much overflowing with the work she should be doing instead. Still,

there was a lot to be said for gazing across the piece of furniture at him instead of down at a pile of bills and invoices. And, she had to admit, the rosemary-wheat and orange-cinnamon breads had turned out very nicely today.

"You know," Sean said after swallowing a mouthful of the former, "not that I'm knocking the vegetarian lifestyle you hold so dear, but... It wouldn't kill you to include some deli-type stuff here at The Harvest, Autumn. Ham, turkey, maybe a little tuna salad or something."

She smiled wanly. "It wouldn't kill *me*," she agreed, "but it would kill the pig, the turkey and the tuna."

He rolled his tongue in the side of his mouth but, judiciously, said nothing.

"Don't worry," she said mildly. "I don't hold your meat-eating activities against you. In fact," she added generously, "some of my best friends are carnivores."

He studied her in silence for a moment more, then, "Mmm," he replied noncommittally.

Still, she couldn't quite help herself when she smiled again and told him, "Even if you must admit that it *is* rather primitive behavior."

Her comment, for some reason, really seemed to capture his attention. Because that blue heat that had shone so brightly in his eyes earlier suddenly returned. Tenfold.

"Primitive behavior, huh?" he asked. He continued to contemplate her for another thoughtful moment, then, "You know, Autumn, there's a lot to be said for primitive behavior. Don't knock it till you've tried it. There are plenty of people who actually *enjoy* primitive behavior from time to time."

She feigned shock. "Really? I can't imagine why."

No sooner had the words left her mouth than Autumn found herself being scooped up out of her chair by Sean and settled ignobly on her...desk. As she scrambled to find the proper words of outrage to utter, he wedged himself in between her thighs and roped his arms around her waist. And then, as she gaped at him in complete surprise, he grinned devilishly, crooked his head to the side and leaned forward to cover her mouth with his.

Primitive, indeed, Autumn thought vaguely, warmly, as she melted into his kiss. Well, what else was she supposed to do? Her entire body had been on red alert ever since she'd seen Sean standing in the shop, and the warning fires had only burned hotter and brighter with every passing moment. Right now, for the first time that day, that week, that month, Autumn began to understand why she'd gotten out of bed this morning. So that she might feel like…like…like *this.*

Excited. Enraptured. Anticipatory. *Alive.*

Because that was exactly how Sean Monahan made her feel. Alive. For the first time in years. With one simple look he'd awakened parts of her she hadn't realized were lying dormant. With one touch he'd set fire to parts of her she hadn't known could even feel warmth. And with one kiss, that wonderful, delicious, overwhelming kiss of the night before, he'd made her remember something she'd forgotten, something very important. He'd made her remember what it felt like to be a woman.

She had no idea why, or how it had happened, only that there was something about him, something *in* him, that provoked a response in her unlike anything she'd ever felt before. And she was no more capable of halting that response—or resisting that response—than she was able to stop the sun from rising in the morning.

So she lost herself in this kiss, too, telling herself it was the right thing to do. It did feel so good, after all. And so right. And it would only be for a little while. She had to go back to work soon. Very soon. She did. And there were people right on the other side of that door, that *unlocked* door. So there was no danger of things between her and

Sean progressing too far. No danger at all. None whatsoever. Not one iota…

Oh, my…

The arms he had wrapped so tightly around her waist
began to loosen some, but instead of releasing her, Sean
only pulled her closer, opening one hand over the small of
her back and letting the other wander freely over her shoulder blades and her nape, up along her throat, finally cupping
it around her jaw and chin. With a gentle exertion, he used
that hand to tip her head backward and urge her mouth
open wider, then he plunged his tongue inside, tasting her
deeply, passionately, totally.

Instinctively Autumn lifted her hands to his hair, cupping
one over the crown of his head, threading the fingers of the
other through the silky tresses at his temple. For a moment
she thought about vying with him for possession of the kiss,
but it felt so good submitting for now, that she decided she
was right where she wanted to be. Sean seemed to sense
her subtle surrender, because he emitted a rough-sounding
rumble and deepened the kiss even more.

The hand on her jaw loosened then, dropped to her neck,
her collarbone, the sensitive cleft at the base of her throat,
then lower still. As he continued to kiss her, she felt his
fingertips skimming along the scooped neck of her blouse,
back and forth, back and forth, back and forth, each stroke
shortening bit by bit, until he turned his hand around at the
entrance to the valley between her breasts, and brushed the
backs of his knuckles gently up and down over her heated
flesh.

Oh, that felt…so good.

And then, very slowly, as if he wanted to give her ample
opportunity to stop him, he dropped that hand lower still,
rubbing the backs of his curled fingers over the plump swell
of her breast nestled beneath the soft cotton of her blouse.
And then yet lower, more slowly, until he was skimming

the backs of his knuckles over her quickly ripening nipple, again and again and again, until Autumn thought she would go mad with wanting him.

She didn't notice that he had stopped kissing her until she realized how hard she was breathing. Or maybe he was the one who was breathing hard, she thought vaguely, feeling the damp heat of his breath as it stirred a few errant curls at her temple. Oh, yes, they were both definitely having a bit of trouble in the breathing department right now.

Slowly she opened her eyes, only to find him gazing not at her face, but at the hand he was dragging resolutely over her breast. His cheeks were ruddy with his desire, his eyes dark with his wanting.

"Sean."

She hadn't planned on saying his name aloud, especially in such a ragged, tempestuous voice, a voice she scarcely recognized as her own. But the moment she did, he lifted his gaze to hers, and what she saw in his eyes nearly stopped her heart. She was about to say something more—though, truly, she had no idea what—when a quick trio of raps at her office door halted her.

"Autumn?" Tiffany's voice called out from the other side of the door. "It's starting to pick up out here. We could use you out front."

Immediately Sean sprang away from her, and Autumn leaped down from her desk. "I—I'll be, um…I'll be right there," she called out to her employee, hoping she only imagined the trembling in her voice. To Sean she had no idea what to say.

He, however, seemed not to have that problem, because after a few more irregular breaths he said, "See? I told you. There's a lot to be said for primitive behavior."

And as much as Autumn wished she could disagree, she had to admit that he was right.

Eight

As providence would have it, Sean ultimately did end up having to follow his original plan that day, because after that much-too-brief but nowhere-near-satisfying encounter in her office, Autumn was simply much too busy to see him. Or to converse with him. Or to even wait on him, much to his irritation. Even after he spent much of his afternoon hanging around the bakery, drinking enough coffee to keep a small, sovereign nation awake for weeks, waiting for a break in the action so that he might exchange even a handful of words with her, not a single opportunity arose. Office encounters aside, weekends, clearly, were not a good time to try and make time with Autumn Pulaski.

Sean adjusted his plan accordingly.

And good thing, too, because when he tried to alter his plan again the following day by stopping in at the bakery— just to say hello, honest—he was forced to realize that Sundays were even more hectic at The Harvest than Saturdays were. Autumn was working hard enough for ten people that day, so hard, she barely managed a wave in greeting to Sean, and she certainly wasn't able to spare much more than a ''What can I get for you?'' followed quickly by a ''Come back soon!''

Come back soon, he echoed to himself after Autumn said it. *All right then,* he thought, *I will.*

He could scarcely believe his extreme good luck on Monday morning when he went to The Harvest—Autumn had, after all, told him to come back soon—and found that Monday was the one day of the week when the place was closed. He rubbed his hands together with much satisfaction—nay, with much glee—at the discovery. If the bakery was closed, then Autumn must be at home. And if Autumn was at home, then this early in the morning she must almost certainly be in bed. Especially after the kind of weekend she'd had.

Yes, in bed was no doubt where he would find her at that very moment, he decided happily. That lush, cozy, perfectly sized-for-two, impossibly feminine bed. That bed where Sean had imagined making love to her on many, many occasions. He had both imagined it on many, many occasions and in those imaginings he had made love to her on many, many occasions. And he was certain that that very bed was where she would be right now.

He made a slight adjustment to his plan.

And within fifteen minutes he was standing at Autumn's front door, lifting his fist to rap as loudly as he could. He didn't want to ring the bell, because he knew what a jolt to the system that could be early in the morning. His brother Finn, workaholic early riser that he was—grumble, grumble—delighted in stopping by Sean's apartment on his way to work in the morning, ostensibly to spend some quality time with his favorite brother. Sean, however, knew it was really just to wake him up long before any normal human being would usually awaken—say at 11 a.m. or so—because Finn did, after all, make it his life's work to annoy him.

At any rate, Autumn, Sean was confident, was a sound sleeper, thanks to all her hard work, and he didn't want to awaken her with the rude grating of the doorbell. No, he would much rather have her wake up slowly. Gradually. Groggily. Just slowly enough that her judgment would be slightly impaired. Just gradually enough that she would forget to put on her robe when she rose from bed. Just groggily enough so that when she finally did come to answer the door, she would be rosy-cheeked and dreamy-eyed and sleep rumpled. He wondered if she slept with her hair unbound....

He paused before knocking to visualize how she might look, and when, several wildly erotic moments later, he finally got around to thrusting his fist forward, his hand came into contact with naught but air. Because before his fist could land one on the front door, that front door was jerked open from inside.

And then there stood Autumn, dressed for the day in one of those flowered, gauzy, full-skirted dresses she seemed to prefer. Not only was she *not* groggy or sleep rumpled, but she was more bright-eyed and put together than anybody had a right to be this early on a Monday morning. Hell, the only reason Sean was awake was because he'd intended to catch Autumn off guard again. Why was it that she always seemed to be one step ahead of him in that department?

"Oh," she said when she saw him, clearly more than a little startled by his presence. Her amber eyes went round with surprise, and her ripe, red lips formed an almost perfect circle. "Hello, Sean," she finally said.

He took some heart in the fact that she blushed furiously when she saw him, but he was still disappointed that he hadn't gotten to jump on her. Or rather, he hastily corrected himself, hadn't gotten *the* jump on her.

"Uh, good morning," he replied as cheerfully as he could, hoping he managed to mask his disappointment that she hadn't answered the door in some filmy little negligée with her hair streaming down over her shoulders and points beyond, looking rosy and dreamy, and sleepy-eyed and half-aroused, and—

"I stopped by the bakery," he hurried on, before his thoughts could get away from him, "and I saw that it was closed. So I came here instead."

"Why?"

For all its succinctness, Sean thought, that was a very good question. Too bad he hadn't thought that far ahead in his amendment to his plan. If he had, he'd probably have a good answer for the question right now.

"Um," he began eloquently. "Because."

She arched her elegant brows in silent encouragement, so Sean scrambled for some halfway plausible explanation. "I, uh, I wanted to invite you to breakfast," he finally said, thinking it a rather brilliant response, all things considered.

"Thanks, but I've already had breakfast."

Okay, maybe not so brilliant. "Then, um, since it's your day off," he tried again, "I thought maybe we could spend the day together."

She eyed him ruefully. "Gee, Monday is sort of my errand day. I have a lot I need to get done before I go back to work tomorrow."

"I could run errands with you," he offered.

That seemed to surprise her, because she asked another one of those oh-so-succinct questions. "Why?"

He blew out an exasperated breath. "Look, why do I have to have an excuse to hang out with a beautiful woman?"

That, too, seemed to surprise her, because this time she

didn't even ask one of those oh-so-succinct questions. Which made her response even more succinct. So Sean pushed on.

"I mean, really, Autumn, we are dating. Aren't we?"

She began to look nervous for some reason, dropping her gaze down to the porch and fiddling anxiously with the top button on her dress. "Only for a lunar month," she reminded him unnecessarily.

Not that he needed reminding. And not, for a moment, that he believed it. He had much too much planned for them to have it all end in a few short weeks.

"Then let's date," he said pointedly. "It'll be an errand date, how about that?"

"An errand date?" she asked, still avoiding his gaze, clearly not sure what to make of that.

He nodded forcefully. "People go on them all the time. It's the wave of the future in our busy society."

"Oh." She didn't look anywhere near convinced.

"So, come on," he told her. "Where to first?"

But she still didn't seem quite ready to capitulate. All she did was gaze at him curiously, as if she were trying to figure him out.

Good luck, Sean thought. He could barely figure himself out lately.

"An errand date," she finally said again.

He nodded.

"Well, if you really want to tag along…"

"Oh, I really do." At this point, after working so hard to convince her, wild horses couldn't keep him away.

For one more moment Autumn considered him silently, then, finally, she shrugged. "Okay. I'm going to the grocery store first, so I can avoid the crowds. Then I need to hit the post office and then the bank and then the copy shop and then the wholesale supplier's…" She began enumer-

ating her destinations on both hands, each one less interesting and more tedious sounding than the one before it.

"Sounds great," Sean replied blandly as he moved aside
to let her pass. He could hardly wait.

For the two weeks that followed, such was Sean's and
Autumn's lot in life. They dated quite steadily, taking in
as many of the local sights and events as could be found
in a small town like Marigold during the summertime. The
Kiwanis Picnic, the Founders' Day Dance, the grand opening of a new restaurant called Peg's Diner, the dedication
of the new hospital wing, and another double feature at the
Skyway Drive-In, which Sean had been certain was supposed to be the *Hot Bikini Nights Marathon,* but which
actually wound up being a Julie Andrews double feature
instead.

And every night that they went out, Sean behaved like
a perfect gentleman when he took Autumn home. Okay, so
maybe there were occasions when he behaved like a perfect
gentleman in heat, because some of their lingering good-
night kisses went way beyond the *lingering* stage.

That was beside the point. The point was that Sean considered himself to be quite the successful dater of Autumn
Pulaski, the town's most-sought-after datee. In fact, putting
all modesty aside—which was always easy for Sean to
do—he was reasonably sure he was the *most* successful
dater of Autumn Pulaski in the history of Marigold, Indiana. In fact, considering the rate at which he was wooing
her—and the rate at which she was responding to that wooing—he was confident he could convince her to stretch their
one lunar month together into two. Maybe three, if he were
feeling particularly magnanimous by the end of that second
one. He would have to wait and see.

But her responses to his very enthusiastic wooing were,
well, very enthusiastic indeed. The two of them spent a

goodly number of evenings sitting on her patio, enjoying after-dinner coffee, or relaxing on her porch swing, enjoying a glass of wine, or standing entwined on her darkened front porch, enjoying each other. And when it rained, they moved indoors. Over those next two weeks, their good-night kisses gradually built from brief, poignant farewells to red-hot, can't-wait-to-see-you-agains. But never once did he—or Autumn—overstep the bounds of propriety.

More's the pity.

Which was how he found himself to be tangled up with Autumn one balmy summer evening three weeks and two days into their relationship and feeling frustrated as hell. And it *was* a relationship—Sean didn't fear that word the way he had before. Because he understood now that one could, in fact, have a relationship with a woman that was only temporary.

Because what he felt for Autumn went beyond anything he'd ever felt for another woman. Though he was sure it was nothing to get alarmed about. Still, it didn't bother him to call what they had a relationship, because it was precisely that. It just wasn't a *lasting* relationship, that was all.

And that was fine, too. Provided, of course, it lasted two lunar months. Or so. He still hadn't ruled out going beyond the parameters set by his brother Finn. Just for the fun of it, of course. Just because he and Autumn got along so well. Just because she felt so good to hold on to and smelled so wonderfully fresh and tasted like a warm cinnamon bun on a cold rainy morning. That was all.

"You taste so good," he told her now as he nuzzled the soft spot where her shoulder met her neck and inhaled great gulps of her wistful, womany smell.

They stood at her front door, saying good-night after a leisurely dinner and some quiet dancing at Tony Palermo's Stardust Ballroom and Supper Club, where Sean had been surprised to see his brother Rory gallivanting—and *galli-*

vanting wasn't a word Sean used often, especially in relation to Rory—with the local librarian, Miriam Thornbury. Even more surprising, Miriam Thornbury hadn't looked *anything* like the local librarian, but more like Tony Palermo's top dance instructor, Lola Chacha—which, of course, wasn't her real name, but was appropriate nonetheless.

Still, thoughts of Rory paled when Sean recalled the soft, luscious, curvy woman he held in his arms, and he skimmed his open mouth up over her neck, her jaw, her cheek, stirring a few errant wisps of hair at her temple before moving back to her mouth.

"You don't taste so bad yourself," Autumn replied in that low, husky voice Sean had grown to love. Because when her voice was low and husky like that, it meant she was as turned on as he was. Really, he thought, he ought to start thinking more seriously about that seduction business. It had been over three weeks since they started dating, he reminded himself. They were long overdue.

"Autumn," he began.

But before he could get any more words out, she discreetly began to disentangle herself from his arms. "As much as I hate to call it a night," she said, "I really do have to go in."

"So soon?" he objected. Hell, they'd hardly necked at all. They were still standing up straight, for heaven's sake. He'd been hoping he could at least get her at a forty-five-degree angle before they called it a night.

"I have to get up earlier than usual tomorrow," she told him. "I'm going to have to open the bakery by myself. Louis had to go home to Indianapolis for a funeral, and Amber and Tiffany are going to be on a day trip with their church youth group."

Sean gaped at her. "You let your entire staff take a day off?" he asked.

She shrugged. "Well, they all had places they needed to be. It won't be that hard on me. It'll be Tuesday, so The Harvest won't be that busy. I'll just have to get there a lot earlier than usual, so that I can do the baking by myself. Tiffany and Brittany prepared all the small pastries today and put them in the refrigerator. All I'll have to do is pop them into the ovens tomorrow."

"Yeah, but that's still a lot of work for you," Sean pointed out.

"It won't be that bad," she assured him. "A bit hectic, but nothing major."

"I could come in and help you," he offered impulsively, surprising himself. On second thought, though, he realized it might be kind of fun. And, hey, Autumn would be there. What better reason for getting up early?

She seemed surprised by his offer, too. "You'd really do that?" she asked, smiling.

"Sure," he told her, nodding. "That's the beauty of self-employment," he added. "I can give myself the day off if I want to. I'm not working on any programs right now that are pressing. It might be nice to have a change of pace."

She smiled, clearly gratified by his offer, and something told Sean her gratitude hadn't come about just because she wouldn't have to shoulder such a massive workload alone tomorrow. No, clearly she was happy just to be having the company they might keep.

"Thanks," she told him before pressing one final kiss to his cheek. "Then I guess I'll see you in the morning."

"Mmm," he murmured as he pulled her close again, looping both arms snugly around her waist. "In the morning, huh? Should I meet you at the bakery, or do you just want to roll over and nudge me?" he asked playfully.

He knew immediately that he'd said the wrong thing. Because Autumn went rigid in his arms for a moment before deftly extricating herself from his embrace to unlock her front door.

And Sean let her do it, because he knew better than to try and dissuade her of the notion. He'd seen women swept up into righteous indignation a time or two, and that was one feminine condition he didn't want to tangle with. Again.

"Autumn," he petitioned softly as he released her. "I'm sorry. It was a joke."

"Of course it was," she said curtly, pushing the door open, making a move to step through.

But Sean easily circled her wrist with sure fingers, and gently tugged her back out onto the porch. "C'mon," he said. "Let's not end the evening this way."

"I don't know what you're talking about," she said coolly, still not looking at him.

Sean didn't push his luck by trying to pull her into another embrace, but neither did he release her yet. "Look, I'm sorry," he said again. "But you have to admit there's something simmering here between us, and it's been on the back burner way too long. A lot of people would have followed it through to its logical conclusion by now."

Two bright spots of pink darkened her cheeks, the only indication Sean had that she knew *exactly* what he was talking about. Because her other features remained schooled into a perfectly bland expression. "I think you're presuming too much," she said softly.

"And I don't think I'm presuming at all. You'll never convince me that you don't want to take that next step as much as I do."

When she said nothing, he let go of her wrist, but not before leaning forward to press one final, soft kiss to her cheek. "Soon, Autumn," he said as he moved toward the steps, confident she would know what he meant. Just to be sure, however, he threw over his shoulder one last time, "Very, very soon."

Nine

Sean was still half-asleep when he stumbled—quite literally—into the bakery at ten minutes to six the following morning. *Ten minutes to six,* he muttered irritably to himself. *That's the same thing as 5:50.* He squinted irascibly at the bright fluorescent lights overhead and bit back a growl of discontent. *Hell.* He couldn't remember the last time he'd been awake and vertical at this godforsaken time of day.

Oh, wait a minute, he recalled groggily. Yes, he could, too, remember. He'd roused himself this early the morning he'd first formally made Autumn's acquaintance, the morning he'd launched his plan to date her for two consecutive lunar months. His plan had called for catching her off guard that day, to better ensure her acquiescence when he asked her out. Hence the unspeakably early wake-up call that morning.

Sean managed a small smile now when he remembered

how well his maneuver had worked. He really had caught Autumn off guard that morning. Completely off guard. Of course, she'd caught *him* completely off guard, too, he realized. And that hadn't actually been part of his plan.

Still, it had sent him from point A to point B and points thereafter, hadn't it? So the endeavor must have been marginally successful, anyway. Sean figured he was probably up around point M by now—*M* standing for *muttering irritably,* he couldn't help but think. Point S was the point where the actual *Seduction* would take place, he'd decided, so he stopped his irritable muttering and tried to focus on what lay ahead.

What lay ahead, he immediately saw, was Autumn, looking fresh and perky in her baker's whites, clearly as wide awake as a double espresso with a sleep disorder. He halted in his tracks when he saw her, and not just because he was too damned tired to walk any farther—though, admittedly, that had something to do with his lack of motion.

But what had more to do with it was the fact that Autumn was smiling and bustling about the kitchen with deft, easy motions while humming a tune off-key. *Humming,* Sean marveled. Incredible. How anyone could hum at this time of day—how anyone could do anything but quaff great gulps of coffee and try to focus their eyes, their brains— was beyond him.

Then he noticed one of those way-too-big-for-a-refill cups of coffee sitting on the counter near where she was working—and humming—and his smile grew broader. So Autumn Pulaski had trouble waking up in the mornings, too, he thought. Somehow, the knowledge of that sent a warm spiral of pleasure rippling through him.

Then again, that warm spiral of pleasure might *possibly* have been a result of the fact that, just as it started its rippling, Autumn bent over to retrieve something from under the counter, and her full white skirt molded over her lush derriere in a way that made Sean go hard like *that*. Oh, yeah, he was fairly certain that that particular view was the actual cause of the peculiar warmth sweeping through him. Except that as he watched her straighten again, he realized it wasn't a peculiar warmth anymore. No, now it was a hot, raging inferno of need.

And then he realized that the real reason for that raging inferno might be because—speaking of infernos—all of the ovens in Autumn's bakery seemed to be stuck on the bake-it-to-a-crisp setting at the moment. As a result, the temperature in the kitchen hovered around what Sean gauged to be, oh, approximately twelve hundred degrees Fahrenheit. Then again, he thought further still, when he noticed the way Autumn's apron front dipped beneath the low scoop of her peasant blouse, and how the rosy swells of her breasts rose above that scoop, maybe the ovens didn't have anything at all to do with why the raging inferno had come about.

Had he thought he was hard a moment ago? he wondered vaguely. Wow. He'd had no idea.

Doing his best to push aside thoughts of Autumn's rosy breasts—though not succeeding very well—Sean managed a few more, rather awkward, steps toward her. Coffee, he reminded himself. What he really needed now more than anything else in the world was a piping-hot cup of coffee that would jump-start his brain and body parts beyond. Well, his *other* body parts, he meant. The parts that he would actually be *using* today. That one body part, after all, already seemed to be working just fine.

Like Autumn, Sean had somehow found the foresight to dress in white this morning, because, after his few idle trips to The Harvest, he'd realized that white was what all the hip bakers were wearing these days. He'd donned an old pair of white painter's pants, along with a white V-neck T-shirt and sneakers, but he could already tell that at least part of his uniform was going to be coming off soon. Not because he had any illusions of jumping forward in his plan to point S, but because of that previously noted twelve-hundred-degree atmosphere. In fact, that huge cup of piping-hot coffee he'd been looking forward to enjoying suddenly didn't hold quite the same appeal as it had mere moments ago. Because what Sean suddenly realized he was craving was a nice big cup of Arctic tundra instead.

It was going to be a long morning.

"Morning," Autumn said with a smile, when she glanced up to see him approaching.

"Yes, it is," Sean managed. "To some, I guess. To me, this is still night."

She offered him a sympathetic smile and nodded toward the big cup sitting on the counter. "Coffee?" she asked.

"Yes, it is," Sean agreed.

She laughed. "No, I meant would you like some coffee?"

Sean expelled a single, weary, chuckle himself. "Oh. Yes, I would. Thanks."

It occurred to him vaguely that he hadn't quite made it into the polysyllabic stage yet, but he supposed that at this point he should be grateful he was able to complete words and phrases in his native tongue. Then he immediately wished he hadn't thought of the word *tongue*. Because it suddenly reminded him that there were things he wanted to do today—with yet more body parts—that went way beyond point S, and those things just weren't part of his plan.

Then again, he realized, his *plan* hadn't actually been going according to plan much, had it?

It probably would have been an intriguing realization, if not for the fact that Sean still hadn't enjoyed his first cup of morning coffee. Soon, though, his brain was sure to begin processing the information it was receiving, just as well as that other body part was processing information—or something. And then Sean was sure to understand what his realization meant, and shortly thereafter he would no doubt be affected by it. Or, rather, more than one body part would no doubt be affected by it. Because that first body part was still hard just from him standing there gazing at Autumn.

"Coffee," he said quickly, proud of himself both for thinking about something other than seducing Autumn and for using a two-syllable word, both at the same time.

Then she smiled, and that seducing-Autumn business jumped right back to the forefront of his brain.

"Coming right up," she said.

Too late, he thought irreverently. After all, it had been up for a while now. Ever since he'd laid eyes on Autumn. Actually, that wasn't completely true, he thought as he tried not to grin *too* lasciviously at her comment. He'd awakened in this condition not an hour ago, due to a couple of very racy dreams he'd enjoyed last night. Dreams that had, inescapably, featured Autumn. Fortunately, he'd managed to battle those explicit images back to the very edge of his consciousness—until now.

Thankfully, she crossed to the other side of the kitchen then, to where a big, industrial-strength coffee urn squatted on an opposite counter. Sean watched every move she made as she plucked a big cardboard cup from a stack and held it under the stream of dark, steaming brew, listened as she began humming that semimelodic tune under her breath again, inhaled deeply the aromas of fresh dough and cinnamon, could fairly taste the mingling flavors of brown sugar and coffee. Oh, yeah. His senses were definitely coming to life. So far, four out of five were working just fine. Now if he could only do something to double-check that sense of touch....

He had conjured a few very good mental images of ways to do that, when Autumn pressed the cup of coffee into his hand and dissuaded him of pursuing every last one. Not because he could distinctly feel the cardboard against his hand, thereby confirming that his sense of touch was working A-OK, but because the heat beneath that cardboard nearly burned the flesh from his palm, thereby confirming that his sense of touch was now in danger of becoming his sense of never-feeling-anything-again-for-the-rest-of-his-natural-life.

Quickly he set the cup down on the counter and, while waiting for it to cool—which, of course, wasn't likely to happen anytime soon in twelve-hundred-degree temperatures—he plucked lightly at the cotton T-shirt that was already clinging damply to his chest.

"Is it going to be like this all day?" he asked.

Autumn gazed at him, puzzled. "Like what?"

He raked his open palm over the moisture forming on his forehead. "This hot," he clarified.

She nodded. "I'm afraid so. At least, it will be as long as we're baking. But don't worry—you get used to it pretty quickly."

Sean sincerely doubted that. Without even thinking about what he was doing, he reached behind himself to bunch a fistful of shirt in his hand, and automatically began to tug it over his head. When he saw Autumn's expression in reaction to the gesture, though—an expression of, gosh, stark-raving horror?—he hesitated, shoving his shirt back into place.

"What?" he said. "Is there some health law that says I can't work shirtless?"

She shook her head. "No-o-o..." she said with some distraction. "Not really."

"Then what's wrong?" he asked.

She said nothing, only continued to gaze at him in that clearly worried, starkly horrified, way.

"Autumn?" he tried again.

"Nothing," she said quickly. Maybe a little too quickly. "There's nothing wrong. Just…"

"What?"

But she only shook her head again and repeated, "It's nothing. Go ahead. Louis has worked without his shirt from time to time, and no one's said a word about it."

Of course, Autumn thought as she watched Sean tug his shirt over his head and toss it aside, that was because Louis looked more like the cream puffs for which he was famous when he took his shirt off, as opposed to the piece of Greek-god artwork that Sean resembled when he took *his* shirt off.

Oh, it was going to be a long morning.

"You might still want to put on an apron," she told him in a last-ditch effort at preserving her own sanity. If she was going to have to work in close quarters with him, and him being half-naked that way, and his half nakedness looking like…looking like…like…like *that,* then she was going to go mad. "It can get pretty messy," she finally tacked on as a warning.

Especially when you're all hot and sweaty and hot and luscious and hot and sexy, she added to herself. She couldn't see any reason to elaborate like that for Sean. Her gaze was fixed helplessly on the flexing and relaxing of the muscle and sinew rippling over his back and torso, so she had to fumble around blindly on the counter beside her as she tried to locate the apron she'd pulled out for Sean when she'd retrieved her own that morning. When her fingers finally came into contact with it, though, she still couldn't quite divert her attention from the elegant bumps of salient biceps and triceps, and oh, my goodness, what laterals the man had….

"Thanks," he said

For one brief, humiliating moment, Autumn feared she had spoken her appreciation out loud. Then she realized he had taken the apron from her now-numb fingers and had slung it over his head, and that was why he was thanking her.

"Um, you're welcome," she said shallowly.

She still couldn't quite make herself look away from his naked back, though, and the smooth, bronzed skin that bunched and danced with every move he made. Her mouth went dry when she recalled the times she had let her hands and fingers rove over that part of him while he was clothed. What on earth had she been thinking? How could she have possibly denied herself a more intimate knowledge of him? He was beautiful. Glorious. Magnificent. His flesh probably felt like hot, vibrant satin to touch.

She was just about to act on her curiosity, was actually reaching out a hand to stroke a finger along the graceful lines of his upper arm and shoulder, when a buzzer sounded behind her, bringing Autumn back to the matter at hand. The bread. She was supposed to be baking bread. The shop would be opening in a little over an hour, and she and Sean still had a wealth of work to do between now and then. That buzzer meant the almond croissants were ready to come out of the oven, and the trays of garlic-rosemary dough were ready for kneading.

Thank goodness it was Tuesday, she thought. Otherwise they'd never finish everything they needed to do on time. Had it been a weekend morning, there would have been no way the two of them could finish all the baking that would need completing. But since it was the beginning of the week, early-morning traffic would be mostly for coffee and small pastries. And those she had prepared and refrigerated the night before, and they were in the process of baking now.

Most of what she and Sean needed—and kneaded—to do this morning was prepare the dinner breads that customers would come in to buy later in the day. Still, that meant

they had a lot of work ahead of them. Work, she reminded
herself adamantly. Not play. Even if Sean did look just too,
too yummy for words.

She managed to stay focused on the task at hand for
almost thirty minutes, bustling about the kitchen, retrieving
baked goods from the ovens and carrying them out into the
shop. She left the business of dough kneading to Sean, because he seemed so suited to it, and, truth be told, he
seemed to be enjoying it very much. And he was good at
it, too, Autumn had to admit as she watched him, doubling
both hands into fists and pressing them over and over and
over again into the soft, fragrant dough.

And each time he moved, the muscles in his arms and
chest and shoulders flexed and relaxed, flexed…and…re-
laxed, flexed and relaxed, performing an elaborate, if irregular, ballet that Autumn couldn't help but find fascinating—
among other things. At one point, when she returned to the
kitchen from the outer shop, she stopped dead in her tracks
to just watch the movements of his upper body.

His dark hair hung in lank strands over his damp forehead, his cheeks were flushed from the heat of the stoves
blazing behind him, and his apron, limp from the heat,
gaped open over his naked chest. He was leaning forward,
very intent on his work, those muscles going taut then slack
then taut again.

And the kitchen was so hot, and her mouth was so dry,
and he was so very sexy, and such a dark, needful hunger
roared up from somewhere deep inside her. All of a sudden
she realized that her heart was pounding against her rib
cage at a dangerous rate, sending her blood racing through
her body at a dizzying pace. She felt light-headed and over-
heated, and then, somehow—truly she had no idea how it
happened—Autumn was suddenly standing beside him, lifting a hand toward his bare shoulder.

She only wanted to touch him, that was all. She only

wanted to see if his skin was as smooth and warm as she imagined it to be, only wanted to know if the bunching muscles were as alive as they appeared to be, only wanted to know what he would feel like beneath her fingertips. And then she was finding out, was suddenly skimming her fingers lightly over his upper arm, and she knew that yes, his skin was as smooth and warm as she'd imagined it to be, that the muscles were indeed as alive as they appeared to be, that beneath her fingertips, he was hot and hard and strong and male.

The moment she laid her fingers on his skin, Sean snapped his head up to look at her, and Autumn's legs nearly buckled beneath her at the blue blaze of hunger she saw burning there, a hunger that appeared to be as deep and voracious as her own. And suddenly it wasn't enough to be touching Sean. Suddenly, somehow, she found herself wanting to taste him, too. So, curling her fingers more resolutely around his upper arm, she dipped her head to his shoulder and pressed her mouth lightly to the warm flesh she encountered there.

She wasn't sure, but she thought she heard him growl something feral and indistinct under his breath when her lips made contact with his shoulder, but he never shifted his position, only turned his head to watch what she was doing. And after that first light kiss, Autumn found that she was unable to resist sampling a bit more of him. So she dragged her mouth across his shoulder this time, parting her lips, exerting a little more pressure than she had before. This time the sound he uttered was much less indistinct and much more feral, and hearing it set off little detonations from Autumn's belly to her breasts.

And still she wasn't quite satisfied with the way she was touching him. So she darted her tongue out and slid it lightly, damply over his collarbone, once, twice, three times, back and forth, back and forth, back and forth, tasting salt and cinnamon and man, an intoxicating combination that left her reeling, so narcotic was its effect.

And *still* Sean remained motionless beside her, watching her, his breathing rampant and ragged now, his chest rising and falling eagerly with his rapid respiration. Autumn was afraid to look at his face, fearful that if she made eye contact with him, if she saw that he wanted her as much as she wanted him, then she might very well take him right there in the bakery. So she only continued to brush her open mouth over his shoulder and arm, dipping once to the hollow at the base of his throat, then lower still, to the smooth skin of his chest.

She only halted when her lips came into contact with his apron, and she heard herself utter a soft little sound of discontent before she curled her fingers into the fabric and tried to push it away. She moved one hand behind him, to the loose knot at his waist, and jerked it free. And that, finally, motivated Sean to move, with the speed of lightning, and he jerked the offending garment over his head.

And then his chest was gloriously naked, smooth and hot and damp and hers. She pressed her open mouth to his satiny skin again, but this time Sean was anything but motionless in his response. He snatched the white kerchief off her head and ran his hand down the length of her braid, grabbing the end fiercely before he began winding it slowly around and around and around his hand. Little by little, bit by bit, he roped the long braid around his fingers, his hand, his wrist, halting only when he reached the nape of her neck. There, he gave her hair a gentle tug, not painful, but insistent, and when Autumn tipped her head back in response, Sean lowered his mouth to hers.

The kiss he gave her this time wasn't one of his gentle, tentative, exploratory kisses. Instead it was an explosive, demanding, dangerous claiming of her mouth with his. She gasped at the intensity of it, at the command in it, and he took advantage by filling her mouth with his tongue and tasting her to the darkest recesses of her soul. And Autumn realized then that she felt dark. Hungry. Needful. She wanted him so badly she ached with it, and she knew then that there would be no turning back from what was obviously going to happen. Not today. Maybe not ever.

She didn't question her reaction, though, and neither did she fight it. Because something about the way they were at that moment, and the manner in which they had come together, simply felt like it was fated, destined, preordained by some supernatural force that neither of them would ever understand. So she kissed him back, demanded as much of him as he took from her, told him without words exactly what she wanted.

"We gotta get outta here," Sean murmured hotly against her mouth when he finally managed to tear his lips from hers. "Right now, Autumn. I want to make love to you, right now. I need to be inside you, right now. Tell me that's what you want to."

She swallowed hard. "I want you—"

But no other words emerged, because Sean immediately claimed her mouth again, kissing her even more deeply than before. For long moments he consumed her, each kiss hotter and more thorough than the one before it. He kept one hand tangled in her braid, but let the other rove freely over her body. She felt him everywhere, on her shoulders, her back, her breasts, her thighs, her bottom. And in response she did her best to touch every inch of him, too. She raked her fingers over his bare back and shoulders, his chest, his ribs, every solid ridge of his abdomen. She cupped both hands briefly over his fanny before moving one to his front, wedging it between their bodies to locate that part of him she most wanted to explore.

He went absolutely still when she opened her hand over the hard ridge straining against his fly, and she dragged her palm along the heavy length of him, exerting as much pressure as she dared. Again and again she rubbed her hand over him, creating an urgent friction that arced between them both. Sean's breathing now was shallow and frantic, and his grip was like steel when he clamped his hand over her wrist to halt the movement of her hand.

"My apartment is right around the corner," he said breathlessly. "It's either that, or I'm going to make love to you right here, and there's gotta be some health law against that. But I'm serious, Autumn. It's going to be one or the other. Your choice."

It was crazy, what he was suggesting, she thought. They were in the middle of The Harvest's morning preparations, and in less than half an hour, people would be streaming through the front door. There were scores of things baking in the ovens, dozens of piles of dough waiting to be turned into bread. For one practical moment she reminded herself how much she stood to lose financially if she abandoned her work today.

Then she thought about how much she stood to lose elsewhere if she didn't.

"Help me turn everything off," she said. "We can come back and clean up later."

For a moment he only gazed at her, his blue eyes dark with hunger, his pupils wide with passion. Then, slowly, he nodded once. "Get your things," he said softly, roughly. "And don't leave anything behind that you'll need before the day is through. Because we won't be coming back here today, Autumn. That's a promise."

Her breath caught in her throat at the vehemence of his unvoiced intentions. But she, too, nodded once, slowly. Then he released her and reached for the shirt he had cast to the floor earlier. She watched with surprising detachment as he began to turn off the ovens one by one, and ignore everything else that lay out in the open.

And she remembered that only once had she closed the bakery on a day when it was supposed to be open, last winter, when she and her entire staff, along with half of Marigold, had been waylaid by a flu. She still had the sign from that day stuck in the bottom drawer of her desk, and she went to retrieve it now, while Sean finished closing down the kitchen.

Closed on Account of Illness, said the sign she tucked into the window as she switched off the exterior lights. And as she turned to face Sean, to join him in their escape, she tried to console herself that it wasn't exactly a lie. Because she really was closing her shop on account of illness. And she suspected that what she had was something for which there was no cure.

Because Autumn realized then that she had a very bad case of loving Sean Monahan.

Ten

They barely made it to Sean's apartment without consuming each other alive right there on a dawn-washed Elliott Street. Thankfully, though, his residence was, quite literally, just around the corner, and they arrived there within moments of leaving the bakery. Although daylight was creeping up over the earth, the apartment itself was still dark. Autumn made out a few indistinct details in her quick survey of the place, finding it to be an utterly masculine, utterly single abode. Big, boxy furnishings and few accessories, as if he didn't like to clutter his life with inessentials.

For one brief, poignant moment, she wondered if that philosophy extended to herself. Then she focused on the darkness, the indistinctness of the place, and tried not to think about that. Sean left his apartment the way it was when they entered, Autumn noticed, and didn't bother turning on any lights as he entered and closed the door behind them.

He didn't bother with any niceties, either, and Autumn found she was grateful for that. He simply pulled her into his arms without a word and went right to work on her clothing, jerking her shirttail free of her waistband and running his hands up and down her bare back. She returned the favor in kind, fumbling with his shirt and trousers as he jerked her blouse up over her head and pushed her skirt down around her ankles. His outer clothing joined hers on the living room floor, and their underwear made it no further than the hallway.

They almost didn't make it to his bedroom, so heated had their ardor become. By the time Sean pressed Autumn backward, down on her back atop his unmade bed, she was completely naked, as was he. But instead of joining her there, as she had expected him to, he knelt on the floor before her, hooked his hands under her thighs to spread them wide, and dipped his head between her legs. It took her a moment to realize his intent, and only the soft flick of his tongue against that most sensitive part of her finally made clear what he was doing.

"Oh, Sean," she gasped. She wasn't prepared for... He shouldn't... No one had ever... "Oh, *Sean*..."

But those two desperate pleas was all she was able to voice. Because he nuzzled her, teased her, tasted her again and again and again, before slipping two fingers deep inside her slick canal. The twin sensations of mouth and manipulation rocketed Autumn to a place unlike any she'd visited before, and all she could do was twist her fingers restlessly in his sheets as she waited for the ride to end.

But it didn't end, not right away. Sean took his time quenching his erotic thirst, clearly enjoying himself as he sipped and supped upon her. No man had ever pleasured Autumn in such a way, and such an intimacy stole her breath, her words, her thoughts. Under his flagrant ministrations, she became little more than a sentient creature, mindless, heedless of everything except the keen heat wheeling through her. What he was doing to her, what he was taking from her...

She would never be the same again.

She was on the verge of free-falling from some hazy, dangerous, breath-stealing height, when she finally felt Sean's hard, hot body, stretching out alongside hers. He turned her to her side and lay behind her, opening one hand over her belly and one over her breast. He caught her nipple in the V created by his index and middle fingers, rolling it lightly between the two. He dropped his head to her neck, pressed his mouth to her throat, and then, without warning, he pushed himself inside her from behind. In and out, he thrust himself, again and again and again, plunging deeper and deeper and deeper still, his motions quick and demanding and none too gentle.

Autumn immediately caught his rhythm and matched it, darting her lower body backward as he urged his forward. He'd donned a condom at some point, and the ribbed texture rubbing against the highly sensitized parts of her he'd teased and taunted with his mouth earlier set something to humming desperately inside her. And then that something, already clenched tightly, began to clench tighter still, vibrating wildly before uncoiling in a rapid explosion of heat. Immediately Sean went rigid behind her and shoved himself forward, *deep,* one final time. Together they cried out in the culmination of their union, together they exploded, and together they slowly, gradually unwound.

The moment Autumn relaxed, he turned her toward himself, settling her on her back, and covered her mouth with his. He kissed her long and hard and deep, as if he were branding her, claiming her, taking a not-so-little part of her inside himself. Then, with very clear reluctance, he pushed himself away.

"Just give me a minute...to clean up," he said softly,

raggedly, as he left her. "And then...then, Autumn, we'll talk."

She nodded weakly, hoping a minute was all it would be. Not because she wanted to talk to him just yet. She had no idea what to say after what the two of them had just shared. But she wanted to feel him close again, *needed* to feel him close. She didn't understand any of what had just happened, but she knew she didn't want it to end just yet. The physical, she told herself. She only wanted the physical right now. His body spooned to hers, her mouth on his, two thoroughly turned-on people joined as one. Instinctively, though, she knew she had gotten so much more. Too much more.

She really would never be the same again.

By the time Sean returned to his bed, a pale scrap of daylight was spilling through his bedroom window. But it hadn't yet crept as far as the bed. His eyes, however, had adjusted to the darkness long ago, and he could easily make out Autumn's shape beneath the covers. She lay on one side of the bed, on her back, gazing at the ceiling, and he couldn't help wondering what she saw there.

Was she recalling the way the two of them had just caught fire together? The way they had burned and branded each other? Did she feel the same way he did? Stunned, amazed, awed? Had that been a first for her, as it had been for him? he wondered further. Not the first time making love—clearly both of them had known what they were doing. But the first time it had felt that good?

Oh, man. He had no idea what to do now.

He'd never imagined that making love to Autumn—or to any woman—could be the way it had been between the two of them just now. And he still couldn't imagine what had come over either of them earlier, at The Harvest. One minute she'd been busily stocking the front of the bakery, and he'd been completely caught up in kneading dough. Then the next minute she'd been standing beside him, dragging a finger along his bare arm.

He'd been startled by the initial contact, but he'd been completely blown away by what he'd noted in her eyes when he looked down into her face. Never before had he seen a woman looking so hungry, so needful. Never before had he reacted with such a hunger and need himself.

And when she'd pressed her mouth to his shoulder...

Sean shuddered almost convulsively at the memory. Involuntarily he closed his eyes, parted his lips and replayed the episode in his mind. Even now, when he recalled what had happened, that same need and hunger roared up inside him again, every bit as fiercely and forcefully as it had then.

He opened his eyes again and somehow found the strength to make his feet move forward, then made his way slowly toward the bed. Autumn glanced over when she noticed his movement, and he hesitated, uncertain of his reception. For a moment she only gazed at him in silence, then, as if she were feeling as uncertain as he, she slowly lifted her hand toward him. Quickly, before she could entertain second thoughts, he covered the remaining distance between himself and the bed. He crawled back up on the mattress and drew her against him, tucking her head beneath his chin, wrapping his arms around her bare back and shoulders.

He hadn't even freed her hair from its braid, he thought with a rueful smile. He'd been so eager to be inside her, had been so close to going off, that he hadn't taken his time to explore her and enjoy her the way he normally did with a lover. Then again, she hadn't exactly tried to slow him down, had she? She'd been every bit as eager and demanding as he'd been himself. Next time, he thought, they could go slower. Next time they could be more tender. Next time they could take their time.

Next time. Oh, no. He was already thinking about next time. And he was more fearful than he wanted to admit that there might not be one.

He felt her trembling then, and tightened one arm around her as he tugged the sheet up over their naked bodies. "Are you okay?" he said softly as he settled the soft fabric around her shoulders.

She nodded. "Yes. You?"

That, Sean decided, was a question he'd just as soon not contemplate right now. Because he very much suspected that no, he wasn't okay, that he probably wasn't going to be okay for some time to come. Nothing like this had ever happened to him before. Nothing. Ever. No matter how turned on he was, he never lost control with a woman the way he had with Autumn. Never. Sex had almost always been great in the past, no matter who he was with, and many times it had been downright phenomenal. But never like what it had been with Autumn. Never like that at all.

And she was a woman who never dated anyone for more than four weeks.

"Sean, I'm sorry I—"

"Shh," he interrupted her breathless, hasty apology, pressing a finger lightly to her lips. He didn't know what she was apologizing for, but he didn't really care. There was nothing either of them had done that called for regrets. "Don't apologize," he told her, skimming his finger lightly over her plump lower lip before dipping his head to briefly kiss her. "I can't imagine why you'd be feeling sorry for anything."

She splayed her hand open over his chest, right above where his heart was beating at an erratic, anxious pace. "But I am sorry about something," she said softly.

Damn. "What's that?" he asked, proud of himself for sounding so unconcerned.

She crooked her index finger and began drawing tiny,

concentric circles over his skin. "You didn't get to, um…
I mean, I didn't do anything for you that, uh…"

He smiled. Oh, was that all? "Believe me, Autumn," he
said, chuckling, "I got everything I wanted."

The playful finger on his chest stopped dead in its tracks.
"Oh," she said, a small, hollow sound. For all its brevity,
however, that soft utterance held a wealth of hurt.

"That wasn't what I meant," he hurried to explain. "I
didn't mean sex was all I wanted from you."

She hesitated only a moment before asking, "And what
is it you do want from me?"

She had to ask, he thought. And now he'd have to answer. Too bad he had no idea what to say.

"I want to make love to you again," he told her, side-
stepping, for now—he hoped—the other answers he didn't
want to consider right now. "And this time," he added
before she could object, "I want to go slower."

"But—"

"Lots, *lots* slower," he told her, cutting off her protest
again. He reached for the band at the base of her braid and
tugged it free, then leisurely began to unbraid her hair.
"And I want to start right now."

The moment Autumn arrived home that night, the very
first second she found herself alone, free from the enigmatic
pull of Sean Monahan, she immediately began to regret the
way she had spent the day. Although her time with him
had been wonderful, incredible, phenomenal, she knew
there was so much more at stake here than simply enjoying
herself and him. Yes, what they had shared together had
transcended any experience she'd ever had in her life—
physically, emotionally, spiritually, you name it. But that
was precisely the problem. Because Autumn understood—
too well—that the reason their joining had been so special
was because she had fallen in love with him.

Really fallen in love with him.

She wasn't sure when it had happened, or how, but sometime over the past three-plus weeks, Sean had come to mean more to her than anyone else in her life. She wasn't sure if that had happened the day she'd met him or if it was something that had developed gradually over time. But she did love him. She realized that very well. Her plan, her lunar-month plan, the one she had thought so foolproof and unbreakable, had failed miserably. She simply hadn't counted on someone like Sean when she had developed it.

She hadn't counted on falling in love. Not like this. Never like this.

But what Autumn felt for Sean was infinite and immeasurable. It went way, way beyond those small, tepid feelings she'd held for her ex-fiancés, feelings that were laughably insignificant in hindsight. And she'd been ready to *marry* them, she recalled now, shocked. She had fully planned to spend the rest of her life with men she now understood she hadn't even been close to loving.

It was a sobering realization, to say the least.

What was worse, now that she did understand what love truly was, she was forced to realize that she'd found it with someone who would never return the emotion. Not with the undying, inescapable depth that she gave it herself. Because although Sean Monahan was everything she'd ever hoped to find in a mate—intelligent, funny, good-natured, handsome—he wasn't one for settling down with one woman forever.

He wasn't one for settling down with her.

Oh, what was she going to do?

She leaned back against her closed front door, listened to the sound of Sean's engine as he drove away, then dropped her head miserably into her hands. Outside, the moon was up and the stars were out, and it was an incredibly romantic night for lovers. But she had kissed Sean

good-night on her front porch, had given him some vague
reassurance that yes, of course she would see him again
tomorrow and had darted inside her house and bolted the
door behind herself.

She'd behaved so unlike herself today. First, by closing
the bakery the way she had—she'd lost a good bit of in-
come doing that and had been totally irresponsible. But
what had been even more irresponsible was succumbing so
completely to her rampant needs and her errant desires in
the first place. Yes, she had wanted Sean more than she
had ever wanted anything, or anybody, in her entire life.
But she was an adult woman who knew better than to allow
her whims to overtake her. She'd been stupid today, letting
herself go wild the way she had. And now she was going
to be paying for it for a long, long time.

Sean had wanted to go back to the bakery before bringing her home, to help her clean up, but Autumn had assured
him that she and the others would be able to manage it in
the morning. There was no way she trusted herself to be
alone with him any longer than she already had been. Already, she'd assembled a suitable lie to tell her employees
tomorrow, about how she'd come to work and gotten halfway through the morning preparations before succumbing
to some mystery ailment that had caused her to close the
place down, as well as she could, and rush home to retire
to bed.

She told herself the explanation wasn't all that far from
the truth. Because she had succumbed to something mysterious, and she did feel sick right now, and she had spent
the day in bed. She felt her face flame and her body flush
with warmth as graphic recollections of how she'd spent
that day in bed paraded through her head. Never in her life
had she enjoyed the kind of fireworks that she and Sean
had generated together. She'd had no idea it could be like

that with a man. She'd had no idea how intensely her body could respond, nor how deep her emotions could run.

Oh, what was she going to do? she asked herself again. She couldn't believe she had done it a third time—had fallen head over heels for a handsome, charming, eligible man who had no intention of pledging himself, or his life, to her. Sean Monahan was famous in Marigold for his various girlfriends, his numerous conquests, and his complete inability to ever take anything, especially relationships, seriously. It was one of the reasons she hadn't seen any harm in going out with him. She'd been so sure she wouldn't ever fall for a man like him, and she'd known full well he wouldn't fall for her.

Yet fallen she had. Hard. She'd been completely wrong about herself in that respect. And all too right about him.

Fool me once, she thought, *shame on you. Fool me twice, shame on me. Fool me three times...*

She sighed heavily as she dropped her hands back to her sides, then straightened herself to her full height and squared her shoulders as best she could. *Fool me three times,* she thought again, *and I go on the offensive.*

She would not be defeated by this, she promised herself. She'd been in love before—twice, even—and she'd gotten over it both times. Eventually. She just wouldn't think about how what she'd felt for her two ex-fiancés was totally, utterly, completely lame in comparison to what she felt for Sean. She could handle this. She could. But she would have to handle it alone. They were practically at the end of their lunar month together, anyway. She could just go ahead and break up with Sean now, before things went any farther than they had.

She just wouldn't think about how things had already gone way too far, certainly much farther than she'd ever suspected they would, infinitely farther than she'd ever imagined they could.

There was only one thing for it, she decided bravely, lifting her chin a fraction more. She had to look toward the future and focus on that.

The immediate future, at any rate, she amended much less bravely, dropping her chin a notch. If nothing else, she could go clean up the bakery now, this evening, before anyone arrived tomorrow morning. After all, it wasn't as if she would be getting any sleep tonight. Or ever again. And, hey, cleaning up the mess she'd left at the bakery might take her mind off of Sean Monahan for a while. For, oh, five or six minutes, at least.

And if she had to think about Sean—which, indeed, she knew she must—then doing it while she was cleaning up the bakery would be a perfect time, analogically speaking. She could start rehearsing what she would say to him tomorrow, when she went to tell him that their time together had come to an end. The completion of the lunar month was less than a week away, after all. Sean knew it was coming as well as she did. He couldn't possibly object to her cutting it short by mere days.

Could he?

Eleven

Sean was deeply immersed in his work when he heard the sound of his doorbell the following evening. So deeply immersed, in fact, that whoever was ringing the bell was fairly leaning on it by the time he registered the harshly grating—and constant—buzz. But he ignored it for as long as he could and continued to sit in front of his computer, working feverishly to complete the phrases and graphics that were threatening to flee his brain any moment. Because too many times already today, his thought processes had been interrupted, and, as a result, he'd lost whatever little tidbits he had intended to include in the design of his latest game.

Dammit. He'd just lost another one, too, thanks to the doorbell's incessant grating.

Oh, well. He supposed he should be thankful that it was something concrete interrupting him this time, instead of wayward daydreams about Autumn. *Erotic,* wayward daydreams about Autumn, at that. *Explicit,* erotic, wayward daydreams about Autumn.

Then again, why should he be thankful it was the door-bell interrupting him this time, when it could have been explicit, erotic daydreams about Autumn instead?

"I'm coming!" he shouted at his unseen visitor as he padded barefoot over the hardwood floor to answer the door. "Keep your pants on," he mumbled further as he then yanked it open. When he saw who stood on the other side, however, he immediately regretted the admonition. "On second thought," he told Autumn with a smile he just knew was lascivious—he knew that, because what he was feeling was lascivious, "you don't have to keep them on if you don't want to. Come on in."

He saw right away, though, that his request was inappropriate. Not just because Autumn was wearing a full, flowered skirt and pale-yellow blouse instead of pants, but also by the much-too-anxious expression on her face. Still, he knew what to do to get rid of the latter. And if he did it correctly it would almost certainly go a long way toward getting rid of the former, too.

Without a word he pulled her over the threshold and into his arms, then covered her mouth with his as he pushed the door closed behind her and pressed her up against it. Then he crowded his own body into hers and deepened the kiss, splaying both hands over her ripe, rounded hips, crushing her lush breasts against his chest.

God, he'd forgotten how good she felt, all soft and warm and womanly. He could hardly believe fewer than twenty-four hours had passed since he'd last held her this way. Somehow it felt as if a lifetime had come and gone since he'd last seen her, touched her, kissed her.

Autumn seemed to think so, too, because she immediately melted against him, her mouth and body going slack against his. She curled the fingers of one hand tightly into his dark-green T-shirt, cupped the other hand over the denim covering his butt. Instinctively Sean pushed his hips forward, rubbing them languidly, intimately, against her, and she uttered a wild little sound in response.

He would never get enough of her. He knew that then. She felt too good, responded too readily, made him feel too many things he'd never felt before. Somehow he would keep seeing her beyond her lunar month. But not because Finn had challenged him to. His bet with Finn was nothing more now than a scant shadow of a memory that barely registered in his brain. Certainly he was grateful to his older brother for being the impetus for this whole thing. But Sean wasn't in it to prove a point anymore. Sean was in it to be with Autumn. And somehow, he was sure, too, that he would keep seeing her beyond his two lunar months. Way, way beyond. He couldn't even think about ending this yet.

For long moments they remained so entwined, greeting each other after such a long absence, silently communicating just how unbearable that absence had been. He felt her fingers tangling in his hair, and he remembered how silky and sensational hers had been the day before, cascading over both their bodies as they made love.

That memory, and the feel of her in his arms, made Sean go hard as a rock, and he moved a hand greedily from her hip to her waist, to her ribs, to her breast. He filled his hand with her, thumbing the stiff peak to life beneath the fragile fabric of her blouse and the delicate lace of her brassiere. Then he dipped his head to her neck, her throat, her collarbone, tasting every inch of her warm, sweet flesh along the way.

He had just unfastened the third button of her blouse, had just pushed away the soft fabric to reveal the even softer, champagne-colored lace beneath, when she suddenly went rigid against him. Not rigid in a good way that told him she was very much enjoying what he was doing to her, but rigid in a startled, almost fearful way. Immediately Sean halted his explorations, and reluctantly he pulled away far enough to gaze down into her face.

Fear, definitely, he saw there. And something else, too, something that caused him even greater alarm. "Autumn?" he said softly. "Is something wrong?"

She nodded slowly, but didn't say anything at first to answer his question. She only gazed at him with wide, hungry, hurt-filled eyes, and he couldn't imagine what could have caused such a reaction in her. Everything had been going so well between them. Hadn't it? She'd been enjoying their embrace as much as he had. Hadn't she?

Hadn't she?

"What is it?" he asked. "What's wrong?"

For a moment he thought she was going to try evading him again, but she finally said, slowly and clearly, "I can't see you anymore."

She might as well have just slammed a two-by-four into his gut, Sean thought, so painful and visceral was his reaction to her statement.

He hid it well, though—he hoped—when he asked softly, "What are you talking about?"

"I can't see you anymore," she said again. But she added nothing to that stark remark, didn't elaborate at all, as if what she'd told him were explanation enough.

Yeah, right.

But all Sean could manage by way of an objection was a halfhearted, "Autumn…"

He told himself he did not sound uncertain and desperate and scared, even if each of those words described exactly what he was feeling inside. She couldn't see him anymore? he wondered. After what the two of them had just discovered together? After what the two of them had shared yesterday? What the hell was she talking about? Where the hell was this coming from?

"I'm sorry, Sean," she said, avoiding his gaze. "But this can't be a surprise to you."

He arched his dark brows in complete disbelief. "A surprise?" he echoed. "No, it's not a surprise. A total shock to the system, maybe, but not a surprise."

She swallowed visibly and continued to focus her gaze on something over his left shoulder. And when he ducked his head into her line of vision in an effort to force her to meet his eyes, she simply shifted her attention to the right instead.

"You knew about my rule," she reminded him. "You knew about it from the start. Our lunar month together will be up in less than a week."

"Yeah, but we still have four days between now and then," he told her. *And the rest of our lives after that,* he added silently to himself. Somehow, he didn't think it would lend much to his argument at the moment, to tell her that. Not because he didn't think Autumn would believe him, but because he could scarcely believe it himself.

Yet that was the realization winding its way through his psyche at the moment. He wanted to spend the rest of his life with Autumn Pulaski. Autumn Pulaski. Of all people. Marigold's resident free spirit. Marigold's resident oddball. Marigold's resident woman who never committed to anyone beyond a four-week time frame.

He reminded himself that that hadn't always been the case with her, that she'd told him herself she'd come close to getting married before on two occasions. But did he really want to marry her? he asked himself dubiously. Dating her for the rest of his life was one thing, but *marrying* her? Wasn't that a bit drastic?

And even if he somehow managed to convince himself that that was what he did indeed want to do—and he wasn't any too sure he could convince himself of that—would she believe him? She'd already been left at the altar twice. That was what had inspired her to make her cockamamie lunar-month rule in the first place. Would she risk being left at the altar a third time?

Not that it would necessarily happen a third time…

Not that Sean could convince himself of that…

This was *not* the way he had envisioned winding up his day. He'd rather thought he might call Autumn once he finished up with his work, and ask her if she wanted to go for a bite to eat, preferably someplace dark and cozy and intimate. Then he'd kind of been thinking they could go back to her place, and then he could make slow, languid love to her all night long in that perfectly sized, impossibly feminine bed of hers.

It was what had kept him going all day…was how he'd coped with having to be separated from her for so long. Now she was telling him that separation was going to last a lot longer than twenty-four hours. She was telling him—

"You can't see me anymore?"

The repeated question sounded stupid, even to Sean's ears, but he had no idea what else to say. It was almost as if his brain refused to process the information.

"No," she said, still avoiding his gaze. "I can't. I'm sorry."

"You're sorry," he echoed, knowing for certain now that he sounded like an idiot parrot, his brain still muddled from what she had just said.

He told himself to play it cool, be detached and not to reveal the depth of his disappointment. Disappointment, hell, he immediately berated himself. What he was feeling went way beyond disappointment. And he was nowhere near feeling cool or detached.

"Yeah, I'll bet you're sorry," he muttered before he could stop himself. "I can tell."

"You knew about my rule," she repeated, still avoiding

his gaze. "You knew this wouldn't last more than four weeks. You knew that, Sean. You knew it."

"What I knew," he retaliated, "what I *know*…"

But his words trailed off before he could complete them, mainly because his thoughts trailed off before he could complete those. There was one thing he did know, though. He couldn't let Autumn end their time together. Not yet. Not like this. But what the hell was he supposed to do?

"Ah, dammit," he grumbled as he pushed himself away from her. He spun around and shoved a hand restlessly through his hair, and wished he could slow the rapid-fire beating of his heart. Wished he could cool the burning sensation in his gut. Wished he could think of something to say that might make her change her mind.

As Autumn watched Sean's reaction, her first instinct was to take back everything she'd just told him. *Hah! Just kidding, Sean! I actually only came over to see if you wanted to go get a hamburger.* But she couldn't quite bring herself to put voice to her second thoughts. Yes, he was acting as if this came as a huge blow, and yes, judging by the expression on his face, by the raggedness in his voice, he seemed as hurt and as hopeless as she felt herself.

Then she realized she shouldn't be surprised by his reaction. She knew he cared for her, knew that he liked her, knew that he wasn't the kind of man who took a relationship like theirs for granted. He'd been sweet and attentive and affectionate ever since they'd started dating.

But that was the way he treated every woman, she reminded herself. He was the consummate ladies' man. He loved women. *All* women. It didn't matter who she was, provided she had two X chromosomes. He'd be reacting this way to any woman who broke off with him. Not because he was emotionally devastated, but because he didn't want to end what he saw as a fun time. Not until *he* was ready to end it himself.

"Sean." She tried again. But she got no further than his name.

Still, that was enough to make him pivot back around, enough to make him look at her, enough to make him look as if he would listen to the rest of whatever she had to say.

She just wished she knew what to say.

"I'm sorry," she finally told him again, knowing it didn't even come close to describing what she actually felt.

He eyed her levelly, motionlessly, for a moment, then nodded, setting his jaw firmly, thinning his mouth into a flat line. "Yeah. I got that part."

She swallowed hard. "I, um, I had a good time," she said softly, lamely.

This time he didn't even nod, only gazed at her as if he had no idea who she was.

"And I, um…I hope we can still be friends."

He squeezed his eyes shut tight, and somehow, she knew that what she had just hoped for would never become a reality. Which was just as well, she told herself. The last thing she wanted to be with Sean was just friends. There was no way she'd be able to pass him on the street one day, wave in greeting, and then pass a few moments chatting with him about the latest Marigold news, and who was dating whom these days, especially Sean Monahan.

That thought brought her up short, reminded her why she was doing what she was doing. Because no matter what, even if she broke her unbreakable, one-lunar-month rule, even if she dared to risk her heart and throw caution to the wind, even if she blindly decided to go for it with Sean Monahan, she knew—she *knew*—that Sean Monahan would never be able to make the kind of commitment she would want from him. That she would *need* from him.

Oh, certainly they might date for some time to come, but Sean wasn't in it for the long haul. He was a man who loved the pursuit, who enjoyed the excitement and anticipation of a new fling and who tired of that fling pretty quickly. Over the two years that Autumn had lived in Marigold, she'd heard enough stories about him and had seen for herself that Sean had the attention span of a thirteen-year-old boy. He'd warmed up more girlfriends over the last two years than Autumn had blueberry muffins.

Of course, she reminded herself, *she'd* dated about that many men....

But it wasn't the same, she told herself now. For one thing, she hadn't *warmed up* anybody, nor had she felt particularly warmed herself—not until Sean had come along. And for another thing, her entire motivation for the frequent change of boyfriends had been to avoid a deep, abiding relationship. Of course, that had been Sean's motivation, too. But where Autumn's reason for her dating habits had been to prevent herself from falling in love and getting hurt, Sean wasn't *able* to fall in love.

Even if it was beginning to appear that maybe he might be able to get hurt.

It was better this way, she told herself. For both of them. Their relationship was bound to end eventually, and she might as well get it over with now. At least Sean would remember her fondly and not recall her as someone he'd grown tired of. And, hey, in a way, she would be special to him. She would be the one woman who had ended their time together before he had a chance to do it first. If that was what it took to make her stand out from the crowd of his other girlfriends, she supposed it would be enough. Because heaven knew he would always be special to her.

"I have to go," she said suddenly.

She remembered then that he had started to unbutton her blouse, and, her cheeks heating in embarrassment—and more—she hastily acted to remedy that. She glanced up as she fastened the last, uppermost, button, only to find that

Sean was watching her every move with the same sort of attention a hawk might show a mouse.

She felt blindly for the doorknob, grasped it and turned it hard. "I have to go," she said again as she tugged the door open. Not for a moment did she take her eyes off Sean. Not because she didn't trust him, but because she knew this was the last time she would see him up close this way. A cold knot of ice settled in her belly at realizing it.

He said nothing, only continued to study her in what was clearly barely controlled silence, with that intense watchfulness that made her feel so cautious.

"I'll see you around?" she asked in a last-ditch effort to make him say something—anything—in response.

He settled his hands loosely on his hips, his blue eyes blazing. "Yeah," he muttered flatly, his voice edged with bitterness. "You'll see me around. Marigold's a small town, after all. We won't be able to avoid each other completely. More's the pity."

Autumn supposed she deserved that, but she tried not to let her hurt feelings show. "Stop in at The Harvest sometime," she told him.

He nodded brusquely. "Oh, yeah. I'll do that," he replied sarcastically. "First chance I get."

Chance, she echoed to herself as she backed out his front door and closed it quietly behind herself. She fought back tears and tried to quell the trembling that wanted to overtake her entire body. Yes, a chance would have been nice, she thought. For both of them.

Twelve

Three Mondays after telling Sean she couldn't see him anymore, Autumn found herself at home—alone—spending her one day off a week—alone—working around the house—alone. Actually that wasn't quite true. Although she certainly *planned* to work around the house today, she hadn't quite gotten around to starting yet.

In fact, although it was nearly 11 a.m., she was still wearing her sleeveless white cotton nightgown, hadn't bothered to braid her hair and was perched on her sofa reading the newspaper. Or, at least, she was gazing at the newspaper. She really didn't care what it had to say. She really didn't care about getting things done around the house today, either. In fact, all she wanted to do at the moment was go back to bed and pull the covers up over her head and pretend the rest of the world—or, at the very least, her little corner of it—didn't exist.

Because, as had become her habit since breaking up with

Sean, Autumn felt uninspired and uninterested and unmotivated and unhappy. In fact, she felt a lot of *un*things these days. Of course, she knew there was a reason for that. It was because, well, she hadn't seen Sean. Which, naturally, was her own fault, a realization that did absolutely nothing to improve her disposition.

But he had to accept some of the responsibility for her mood, too, she thought petulantly. After all, he hadn't had to take her assertion so literally. When she had told Sean she couldn't see him anymore, Autumn hadn't thought he would take it to mean, you know, that she couldn't see him anymore.

But he really had disappeared from her life. In fact, he seemed to have dropped off the face of the planet. Not that she'd run into him with any amount of frequency *before* they'd started dating, but she had seen him around Marigold occasionally—she had, after all, gone out of her way to avoid him, handsome, charming and eligible as he was. It was especially strange not seeing him now, during the warmer months, when just about everyone in town spent most of their time outdoors. And he did live right around the corner from the bakery. She would have thought she would see him at least once or twice.

But even on those occasions when she'd had to pass right by his apartment—always because she was on her way somewhere else and had no other choice but to take that route, honest—she saw no sign that he existed at all. His truck didn't even seem to be parked at the curb where she had become accustomed to seeing it. He simply seemed to have vanished completely.

Were she a superstitious woman, Autumn might have become worried that she'd somehow magically willed him to disappear. But she was fast beginning to understand that she wasn't so much superstitious as she was, well, stupid. Because only a stupid woman would have fallen in love with a man like Sean Monahan. And only a stupid woman would have let him get away.

But what was she supposed to have done? she asked herself as she sipped her morning coffee and continued to be uninterested in the newspaper. She couldn't have resisted Sean no matter how hard she tried. And, face it, she had been helpless not to fall in love with him. As for letting him go, well… She hadn't had much choice. She couldn't change the essence of who he was. Only Sean could do that. And he just wasn't the kind of man to fall in love forever after. Certainly not with Marigold's resident free spirit. Certainly not with the town oddball. Certainly not with Autumn Pulaski, a woman who defined her relationships by the phases of the moon.

Oh, how she wished she'd never developed that stupid lunar-month rule in the first place. Oh, how she wished she'd just sworn off men completely and never dated anyone. Of course, there were a lot of things she wished these days. That didn't mean any of her wishes were going to come true. On the contrary, her wishes were becoming more and more unrealistic—and more and more unattainable—with every passing day. Today, for example, more than anything else in the world, Autumn wished that Sean Monahan would come to her front door, would vow to love her forever and would tell her he couldn't live without her. But that didn't mean it was going to hap—

Bzzzzt.

She started in surprise at the buzz of her doorbell, her body jerking so much that the newspaper in her lap slid to the floor and a few dribbles of coffee splashed over the side of her cup. She narrowed her eyes suspiciously at the front door and reminded herself that she *wasn't* a superstitious woman. In spite of that, she couldn't quite quell the dizzying pace of her heartbeat as she set her cup on the end table and rose to answer the bell. Because even if Autumn wasn't a superstitious woman, she couldn't quite keep herself from being a hopeful one.

Her already rapid heart rate doubled when she opened the door to find Sean Monahan standing on the other side. And it tripled when she saw the expression on his face, a mixture of yearning and melancholy that she knew only reflected her own features. Other than that, two and a half weeks really hadn't changed him much, she thought. He still had black hair, though it was a bit longer, and he still had those blue, blue eyes, though they looked a bit tired. His faded blue jeans clung to his slim hips and muscular thighs, and his black T-shirt lovingly molded that hard, slender torso she remembered being so satiny and hot under her fingertips.

And just like that a raging need roared up inside her, filling that vast emptiness that had been her constant companion for the past two and a half weeks. It was all she could do not to tug him inside, wrestle him to the floor and make love to him right on the spot.

Damn, how she wished her wishes would come true.

"Hi," she said.

Oh, boy, was that a lame opening.

"Hi," he replied, clearly feeling no more creative than she.

For several long moments they only gazed at each other in silence, as if each was cataloguing every little detail about the other, trying to see if things were still the way they had been the last time they were together, identifying all the little changes that came about with extreme absence.

Autumn was the one who finally broke the spell, by asking, very quietly, "What, um…what are you doing here? Not that I want you to leave, I mean," she hurried on before she could stop herself. "In fact, if you want—" She squeezed her eyes shut tight, forcing herself to shut up before she revealed everything else she'd just been wishing for. "I mean..." she began again. But before she could finish, she gave up. She had no idea what she meant.

"Can I come in?" Sean asked.

She opened her eyes again, halfway thinking she wouldn't see him standing there, after all, so confused was she about whether or not she was imagining things. But there he was when she opened her eyes, right there on her front porch, looking so handsome, so uncertain, so intense. There was no way she could refuse him. No way she wanted to refuse him. Still, something kept her rooted to the spot without speaking. She just couldn't quite bring herself yet to invite him inside.

At her hesitation he added, "Please, Autumn. There's something I need to tell you."

Gosh, unless it's that you'll love me forever and can't live without me, she thought, *I don't want to hear it.*

"Please," he said again, his voice softer this time, his expression more pleading.

He sounded so solicitous, so tender, so dear, her heart began to hammer harder still. She immediately took a step to the side, extending her arm toward the living room in a silent bid for him to enter. The moment he crossed the threshold, she closed the door behind him, then forced her feet forward, crossing to the sofa, seating herself there as she indicated that he should sit in the flowered chintz chair opposite.

He took one look at that chair, then another look at Autumn. Then he immediately traced her steps exactly, seating himself heedlessly beside her on the sofa instead. Scant inches separated them, and she fancied she could feel his heat wrapping around her. Oh, he did smell so good, she thought, all fresh and clean and masculine. She'd forgotten how nice it was to simply be close to him.

"We need to talk," he told her before she could object

to his nearness. Not that she was necessarily going to object.

"I, um, I can't imagine what about," she told him honestly.

He studied her intently for a moment, his eyes dark with longing. Something inside Autumn that had been twisted tight gradually began to ease.

"We left things a little unfinished a couple of weeks ago," he told her.

She swallowed with some difficulty, tried to force her gaze away from his, then found that she was helpless to look at anything but him. "I, um, I thought we finished things up pretty well a couple of weeks ago." Oh, what a lie *that* was. She waited for lightning to strike, then reminded herself she wasn't a superstitious woman. Just a stupid one, that was all.

Sean nodded slowly, a deep sadness darkening his eyes now. "Yeah, well, I can understand where *you* might think that, seeing as how you're the one who did the finishing."

"Sean—"

"But I didn't get a chance to say my piece that day," he interrupted. "And I think the least you can do is let me say it now."

She sighed heavily, told herself that what he was asking for was by no means unreasonable, even if it wasn't what she'd been wishing she might hear.

"I love you, Autumn."

That, of course, was what she'd been wishing she might he—

She gaped at him when she realized that no, in fact she had *not* imagined the words in her head—he had indeed spoken them himself. In spite of her realization, though, "What did you say?" she asked.

His expression relaxed some, his lips curling into a smile. It wasn't a big smile, but it wasn't bad. And it was certainly an improvement over the flat, rigid line his mouth had been only a moment ago. "I said I love you," he told her, even more softly this time. "And I've come to the conclusion that my condition is never going to change." He lifted one shoulder and let it drop again, in a careless shrug that was really nowhere near careless. "Basically," he went on, "I think what I'm trying to say is…I don't want to live without you, Autumn."

Oh, now this was just too weird, she thought. Nobody got all their wishes. Especially not in one fell swoop like this. She was dreaming. She had to be. That was it, surely. She'd dozed off while reading the newspaper, and now she was lying on her sofa, sound asleep, dreaming about the very thing she had been wishing for all along. And just to prove that, as surreptitiously as she could, Autumn reached down to pinch her thigh.

"Ouch," she said in response to the sharp pain that shot through her leg. Okay, so maybe she *wasn't* dreaming.

Sean's eyebrows shot up at her outburst. "Ouch?" he repeated. "That, ah, that wasn't exactly what I was hoping you'd say when I told you how I feel about you."

She shook her head fiercely, once, to clear it of the buzzing that threatened to overtake it. "No, I didn't mean ouch, it hurts that you—" She halted herself before she became even more befuddled than she was already. "I mean, uh…I, um," She sighed with some exasperation and simply replied truthfully, "I don't understand."

He smiled at her again, though this time it was a sad, bereft sort of smile. "Gee. What part of 'I love you' didn't you understand?" he asked. "Or was it the 'I can't live without you' that has you so confused?"

"It's all of it, Sean," she told him. "I don't understand any of it. Forgive me for saying this, but you're just not the kind of man who says these things. You're not the kind of man who *feels* these things."

He nodded slowly in what looked like resignation, then let his gaze shift to some point beyond her. He was obviously seeing something that wasn't there, though, when he told her, "A couple of months ago I would have agreed with you there. But a couple of months ago I didn't know you. Not the way I know you now."

"I don't see how that would make any difference."

He expelled a single, humorless chuckle and turned his attention back to her face. "You don't see how that would make a difference?" he asked incredulously. "Autumn..."

He studied her long and hard for a moment, as if he were weighing very carefully what he wanted to say. Then he reached over to cover her hand with his, hesitating only a moment before turning it over toward his, and lacing their fingers together, palm to palm. His skin was warm and smooth against hers, and she realized then that she'd almost forgotten how good it felt just to touch him. Without even thinking about what she was doing, she curled her fingers more intimately with his and held tight.

And for the first time in weeks, she started to feel as if she was alive again.

"Do you know why I started dating you?" he asked suddenly, scattering her ruminations—for now. "Do you know why I asked you to go out with me in the first place?"

She shook her head slowly. "No. Actually, I always did kind of wonder what you saw in me. I mean, not that I'm a horrible ogre or anything, but I'm not exactly like the women you usually date."

He smiled. "You noticed the women I usually dated?"

Oops, she thought. *Caught.* "Um, actually, what I noticed was you," she confessed. "A long time ago."

His eyes fairly sparkled at her admission, but he said nothing, as if silently encouraging her to continue with her confession. Autumn, however, wasn't quite ready to spill her guts that completely. Not yet.

"So why did you ask me out?" she said instead.

He sighed heavily, clearly disappointed that she hadn't revealed herself totally. "Because my big brother, Finn, dared me to," he said.

She narrowed her eyes at him in confusion. "Now I really don't understand."

"I didn't ask you out because I thought you were beautiful and desirable," he told her. "Though, certainly I've always thought you were a beautiful, desirable woman," he hastened to add. "And I didn't ask you out because I wanted to get to know you better, either. In fact, if it hadn't been for Finn, I never would have asked you out at all. Hell, Autumn, I was like the rest of Marigold. I thought you were a—"

"Free spirit?" she finished for him, her heart sinking some at the realization.

This time Sean was the one to shake his head. "Oddball," he told her frankly. "I thought you were kind of weird, Autumn. That's why I never asked you out. Until Finn challenged me to."

Oh, why couldn't she be dreaming now? Autumn wondered. This was the last thing she wanted to hear. "Why are you telling me this?" she asked, unable to mask the hurt that laced her voice when she posed the question.

"Because I need for you to know that I never, ever, planned on this happening."

"On what happening?" she asked, still sounding miserable. Still feeling miserable.

"I never planned on falling in love with you," he said.

Wow. She hadn't dreamed that part, after all. Her mouth dropped open in astonishment at hearing him say it twice. There could be no mistaking it now. Nevertheless, "You...you what?" she asked.

"I've fallen in love with you, Autumn," he said again. "God knows I didn't plan for that to happen, but it did. Big-time. I love you. And I don't want to lose you. Ever."

She gazed at him in silence, still confused, still not sure what to think. So she shook her head in silence, unable to make sense of exactly what she was feeling.

He sighed again, a weary sound, and tried once more to explain. "My brother Finn has spent his life besting me at just about any situation you can name, and it's been a sore spot with me for as long as I can remember. Somewhere along the line in our misspent youth, it became Finn's habit to dare me to do things, and I was always just dumb enough to take him up on it. And always, *always,* Finn came out the winner.

"Then, one night a couple of months ago, a bunch of us guys were talking, and your lunar-month rule came up, and to make a long story short, Finn ended up daring me to date you longer than a lunar month. Me being the arrogant SOB that I am, I told him I could be the man who would make you break your own rule. In fact, I could date you for *two* lunar months."

"So that's how this all started?" Autumn asked. "Your brother challenged you to date me for longer than my rule stipulated?"

He nodded.

Now she was really confused. "But you didn't," she said, putting aside, for now, her realization that she'd once been nothing more to him than a goal to be achieved in a game of I-dare-you. "Even after I broke up with you, you didn't try to change my mind. You lost the dare."

"That's right," he said. "I did. Because at that point Finn's challenge was the last thing on my mind. I couldn't care less if I lost the dare. Because you'd become a lot more to me than that."

"But—"

"Look, I behaved very badly, Autumn," he said. "I never should have accepted Finn's challenge, never should have viewed you like that. But the fact of the matter is, I stopped viewing you as anything but a beautiful, wonderful, intelligent, funny woman immediately after I met you. And at some point along the way, I fell in love with you."

He reached over to take her other hand in his, scooted toward her to close what little bit of space was left between them, and told her, "I don't mind losing to Finn, Autumn. But I don't want to lose you. Ever."

For a long moment Autumn could do nothing but gaze at him, so dumbstruck was she by what he had just said. Then, finally, "Oh, Sean…" she murmured.

She released both of his hands, but only long enough to throw them around his neck and pull him close. Then she buried her face in the warm curve where his shoulder met his neck, nuzzled the rough, fragrant skin she encountered there and murmured something incoherent and delirious.

Sean took it to be a very good sign.

Oh, God, he'd been so scared of what his reception would be when he came here today. He'd been so afraid that Autumn would tell him to take a hike, that she wanted no part of a man who would only date a woman because someone challenged him to, whether he'd fallen in love with her or not. And, frankly, he wasn't sure he could have blamed her if she had told him to shove off. But, scared or not, he'd come anyway. He'd had to. He couldn't live without Autumn. It was that simple. He'd had no choice but to come here today. And now, of course, he was glad that he had. Oh, boy, was he glad.

Oh, boy, was that an understatement.

He roped his arms around Autumn's waist and pulled her close, too, fearful that she might still come to her senses and change her mind. Come to think of it, he'd been fearful about a lot of things for the past couple of weeks. Scared of losing Autumn. Scared she might not return his feelings. Scared she would never forgive him for behaving like an overgrown adolescent. Mostly, though, he'd been scared of what he'd gradually come to understand after she had dumped him. But ultimately, once he'd gotten used to the idea, he was glad he'd finally realized what had happened. He was glad he'd fallen in love.

Fallen in love, he marveled again now. With Autumn Pulaski. Who knew?

Oh, he'd fought it like crazy over the past two weeks. He'd told himself that the reason for his gut-level nausea after she left was only a result of his manly pride being hurt. He'd never been dumped before, had always been the one responsible for ending a relationship before it could go too far. He'd told himself he was just stung because Autumn had beaten him to the punch, that was all.

But then he'd realized that what he was feeling hurt a lot more than a sting. What he'd felt after she was gone was a cold, dark, soul-deep emptiness unlike anything he'd ever felt before. Even then, though, he'd assured himself it was just a temporary affliction, that it would disappear completely the moment he made the acquaintance of another beautiful, desirable woman.

Yeah, that was it.

So he'd taken off for Bloomington for a few days, to put a little distance between himself and Autumn. Ah, Bloomington. Home of Indiana University. Land of coeds and sorority houses. The stuff of every man's dreams.

But even after encountering dozens of beautiful, desirable women, Sean had still felt cold and dark inside. He'd still felt empty. In fact, the more women he met, the more he missed Autumn. Because each of the women he met, well... They weren't Autumn. They didn't even come close. And he realized pretty quickly that he didn't want them. None of them. He wanted...

Hell, he wanted Autumn.

And he wanted her forever.

As he pulled her closer now, he moved his hands to her back, splaying his fingers wide over the soft fabric of her nightgown. God. Her nightgown. She was still wearing her nightgown. Her soft, white, filmy, sexy, barely there... Where was he? Oh, yeah. Her nightgown. Her nightgown and...nothing more?

Well, well, well.

He skimmed his hands lightly up, then down, then left, then right, his fingertips encountering nothing but the silky tresses of her hair and the fragile cotton of her gown. Nope. She didn't have a stitch of clothing on underneath it, he realized, going hard at the knowledge. He dipped his hands lower still, brushing his fingers lightly over her hips and the soft curve of her fanny. Not even panties, he noted, fully aroused now. Goodness, but that was convenient. Not to mention thoroughly and utterly erotic.

In response to his deft touches she nestled her hips more intimately into his hands and murmured something else against his neck—something Sean couldn't quite understand, but which he was fairly certain he comprehended. Just to be sure, though, he asked, "What was that you said?"

She drove her fingers into the hair above his nape and pulled her head back far enough that she could gaze into his eyes. Her own eyes sparkled like vibrant amber, so clear and beautiful were her feelings for him. "I said, 'I love you,'" she told him. Her fingers tightened momentarily in his hair. "Oh, Sean. I love you so much."

And he could see for himself, just by looking at her, that she was telling him the truth.

"You're not mad at me because I only started dating you on a dare?" he asked, still not quite able to believe what was so very obvious.

She smiled. "Hey, it's a better reason than why some men started dating me."

His own smile fell some. "I'll pound to a greasy pulp each and every man who has ever laid a hand on you," he vowed romantically. "Starting with Chuck Nielssen."

Her smile grew broader. "They meant nothing to me," she assured him.

"You're damned right they didn't."

She laughed softly. "No, I'm not mad at you for why you started dating me," she finally said in reply to his question. "I'm just glad you came to your senses and fell in love with me, that's all."

"Yeah, well, I don't think my senses had anything to do with that," he told her.

"No?" she asked innocently.

He shook his head. "Nope. That was my heart that was behind that. My heart, and maybe my—"

She laughed again and halted his avowal with a kiss. A long, lusty, lingering kiss. The kind of kiss that Sean could really get into. So, of course, he did.

He wove one hand through the heavy mass of her hair, until he could cup the back of her head in his palm and tilt it to the side, giving him all the access to her that he wanted and required. Autumn willingly surrendered it to him, opened to him with all the eagerness of an urgent lover. Which, of course, was exactly what she was. As was he. How very convenient indeed.

For long moments they took turns trying to consume each other, each stealing control of the embrace from the other, only to give it up again. Their passion quickly doubled, then tripled, then threatened to overtake them both completely. It was then that Sean recalled Autumn's outrageously feminine, perfectly sized bed, the one where he hadn't yet had the opportunity to make love to her, in spite of all his fantasizing in that regard.

With no small reluctance he wrested his mouth from hers. "You, uh," he began with some difficulty, his breathing erupting in rough, ragged spurts. "You're not wearing anything under that nightgown, are you?"

Autumn smiled at him, a dreamy, seductive little smile. "I dare you to find out for yourself."

He chuckled low. "Oh, now that's a challenge I can't resist."

Before he even realized what he had planned, Sean stood, scooping up Autumn with him. She squealed in surprise, but hooked both arms comfortably around his neck, then pulled herself up enough to cover his mouth with hers. Her hair cascaded down over his arms, his wrists, his hands, feeling so incredibly erotic he wasn't sure he'd be able to last the short distance of her hallway. Miraculously, somehow, he did.

She hadn't made her bed yet, and the piles of creamy sheets and throw pillows offered an invitation that was much too tempting to resist. Sean plopped her down at the bed's center without ceremony, then immediately began to undress himself. Autumn watched with unchecked captivation as he divested himself of his clothing as quickly as he could. And she gazed upon his body in wonder when he stood shamelessly naked beside her.

"Hurry up," she told him.

"Okay," he acquiesced.

He snatched up his blue jeans long enough to claim the condom he'd been so hoping would come in handy, then he tossed it onto the nightstand within easy reach. Not that he wanted to hurry things along, he thought. But just in case...

Autumn rose on her knees and spread her arms wide, another invitation Sean couldn't ignore. He came to her readily and knelt before her, wrapped her in his embrace and kissed her long and hard and deep. He filled his hands with her hair, then let them go wandering, and nearly came undone when he felt her fingers exploring him. Her hands moved surely, seductively, over his bare back and buttocks, kneading, pressing, fingering, loving. Only the thin cotton of her gown kept them apart, but there was something so inexplicably exciting about that, Sean couldn't quite bring himself to do anything about it.

Yet.

Instead, he continued to graze the fabric over her skin, moving the soft wisp of white over her otherwise naked hips and thighs and torso. She writhed impatiently against him in a silent demand for him to remove it, and when he still ignored her, she reached for the garment herself.

"No," Sean said softly, halting her from taking it off.

She gazed at him curiously.

"Not yet," he said.

She smiled that seductive little smile again, then he felt her hands go wandering over his body once more. This time they moved to his chest, his shoulders, his arms, his flat belly, then lower, to that part of him that was straining against her own abdomen. She, too, filled her hand with the fabric of her nightgown, then closed both snugly over him, stroking him up and down and back again. She dragged the soft fabric over his sensitive organ, palming the ripe head before retracing her route again. Sean went still at her intimate exploration, his fists tangled in the fabric at her waist. Before he even realized he was doing it, he was skimming the garment higher, up over her thighs, her hips, her breasts, until he could bend forward and close his mouth over one stiff nipple, sucking, laving, consuming.

Autumn cried out softly as he rolled his tongue over and against her, drawing her more fully into his mouth. But she didn't quite cease her own manipulation of him, this time using her bare hand to arouse him, and Sean grew harder and fuller and thicker against her palm.

Finally, when he couldn't stand any more, he reached for the condom and rolled it on, then urged Autumn onto her back on the bed. Instead of removing her nightgown, he simply shoved it up over her waist, her breasts, then knelt before her, spreading her legs wide, wrapping them securely around his waist. Her hair streamed out around her head like a bright sun, and she gripped his forearms with fierce possession. Sean couldn't imagine what he had done that would win him such a prize as she, but he knew he would do whatever he had to, to make sure he never lost her.

"Marry me," he said as he dropped a hand to play at the entrance to her slick canal.

Autumn closed her eyes and sucked in her breath at his ministrations, but she said nothing in reply to his verbal demand. So Sean upped the stakes, dipped two long fingers inside her, stroking deeply.

"Autumn," he said softly. "I love you. Marry me. Please."

She lifted her hips to greet his deep touch, and Sean buried his fingers as deeply as he could. "Marry me," he said for a third time.

Autumn opened her eyes, and he saw that although her gaze was unfocused and dreamy, her thoughts were right where he needed them to be. "Yes," she told him. "I'll marry you. I love you. Don't leave me."

"I never will," he promised. And he could see that she believed him completely.

"Make love to me now," she told him.

Sean nodded and moved his hands to her thighs, pressing her more open so that he could enter her body with his. Their vows fully cemented, he began to move himself against Autumn, thrusting in and out, deeper and faster, over and over and over again. She quickly caught his rhythm and matched it, driving herself forward with quickening pace, and he moved one of the throw pillows beneath her hips to bring her closer still. Long moments later they both arrived as one at the pinnacle of their release. Together, their fever exploded. Together, they cried out both their passions and their promises. And then, together, they descended back to a reality neither had ever believed would come true.

And some time later, as they lay spent in each other's arms, bathed in the rosy light of a setting sun, they each knew they were exactly where they wanted to be.

"What are you thinking about?" Sean asked quietly, his words a scant murmur as they stirred the hair at Autumn's temple.

She splayed her fingers wide on his chest, holding her palm right over his heart. "I'm just lying here feeling amazed that I started off as a dare."

He chuckled softly and pulled her closer still, folding both arms possessively around her. "I prefer to think of you more as a challenge," he told her.

She laughed, too. "A challenge, huh? Do you still see me that way?"

She felt him nod. "Yep. I do. And I hope that never changes, Autumn. Because there's a lot to be said for challenges."

Epilogue

Christmastime really was a beautiful time to get married, Sean couldn't help but think that third Saturday in December as he gazed into a cracked, faded mirror that hung haphazardly in the church vestry amid robes and sashes. He made one final adjustment to the black bow tie encircling his neck over the crisp white collar of his tuxedo shirt, then turned to face his four brothers-slash-ushers, who were likewise formally decked out. Outside the tiny window behind them, the sun was dipping low over the trees, bathing Our Lady of Lourdes Catholic Church in a wash of gold and orange light, giving the structure an ethereal, almost beatific glow.

Each of his brothers looked more respectable and sophisticated than Sean had ever seen them looking, and he was grateful that each of them was acting totally out of character by not giving him a hard time. Beyond the vestry, he could hear the soft strains of Bach serenading what he knew was a sanctuary packed to the gills with friends, neighbors, relatives and coworkers. Sean's mother was no doubt sniffling joyfully in the first row, his father grinning like a proud papa, because the first of their sons was getting married. His sister, Tessie, though, had beaten him to the altar by nearly a month.

Autumn's family, too, had arrived en masse two days ago. Now her two sisters and a cousin, along with Sean's sister, were wrapped in crimson velvet bridesmaids' dresses in another room on the other side of the church, waiting for the ceremony to begin. Everything, he thought, was coming together nicely. Everything was exactly as it should be. There was just one thing missing.

The bride.

Nobody knew where she was, or what was keeping her, and frankly, Sean was beginning to sweat. He told himself not to worry, that Autumn had never exactly been known for her punctuality, that brides took forever to get themselves into those elaborate gowns they favored, and that any number of things could be making her late.

Then he was forced to remember that Autumn had never been known for her tardiness, either, nor did she generally go in for the elaborate when it came to fashion, and everybody else who was supposed to be at the wedding—including the rest of the bridal party—had already arrived. The last time Autumn's bridesmaids had seen her, they said, she was at her house, packing up the last of her suitcases in preparation for the honeymoon. She'd told them all to go ahead, that she'd be along momentarily. They'd reluctantly abided by her request, and that had been that.

Sean had telephoned her house twice now, only to have the machine pick up. He had no idea where she might be. But there were still ten minutes to go before they were to take that official walk down the aisle. Ten whole minutes, he reminded himself. Ten whole, long minutes. Ten whole, long, full, interminable minutes...

"Where the hell is she?" he snapped suddenly, unable to keep himself from glaring at his oldest brother and best man. Finn, after all, was responsible for this whole thing. Dammit. He was the one who had challenged Sean to date Autumn in the first place.

Finn held up both hands, palms out, in a gesture of surrender. His elegant black tuxedo was identical to Sean's, except that the rose affixed to Finn's lapel was, like his brothers', red instead of white. "Hey, calm down," he said. "I'm sure she'll be here any minute."

"You're sure," Sean echoed. "Now why does that reassure me not one iota?"

Instead of quaking in fear at Sean's lethal tone of voice, Finn only chuckled happily. Chuckled. Happily. Dammit.

"Oh, don't get your boxers in a twist, little brother," he said. "She'll be here."

"When, dammit? When?"

Finn laughed some more. "Will you just calm down? Jeez, I've never seen you like this."

"Yeah, well, there's a reason for that," Sean muttered.

Finn continued to smile indulgently. "What's that?"

"I've never been like this," Sean told him.

"What?" Finn asked mildly. "Half out of your mind in love with someone you're worried you're going to lose if you don't do something drastic, like marry her?"

Sean nodded. "Yeah. That's pretty much it."

"I know the feeling," Finn said, sobering.

Which was true, Sean knew. Of course, the last thing he wanted to bring up now was Violet Demarest, so he glanced at his other brothers, and found Cullen stifling a chuckle. So he turned his venomous gaze there instead. "And just what the hell are you laughing about, boyo?" he demanded.

"Nothing," Cullen told him, still grinning.

Sean made a face. "Yeah, well, you should talk. I've seen the way Madame Mayor Isabel Trent's got you dancing to a tune."

Cullen gaped at him, two bright spots of color darkening both cheeks. "I have no idea what you're talking about."

"Yeah, right," Sean said. "I saw her sitting out there on the groom's side," he added. "And I saw who ushered her in, too. And," he added ruthlessly, "I saw the look on your face as you ushered her."

Cullen snapped his mouth shut tight and said nothing more.

"Look, Sean," Finn tried again, "stop worrying. Autumn, for whatever mysterious reason, loves you. Ya big lug. She'll be here. Don't worry."

But Sean dropped his gaze to his wristwatch again and wondered where on earth she could be. Just as he was lowering his hand, though, a quick rap sounded on the vestry door. Immediately, Finn leapt to open it, and in tumbled Sean's little sister, Tessie, looking flushed and happy and excited.

"She's here," Tessie said. "Everything's fine. Let's get going."

Only then did Sean realize how much he had feared being left at the altar. Only then did he fully understand how devastated he would have been had Autumn not shown up. Only then did he truly understand the depth of his love for her. Only then did he know how very badly he wanted to join his life to hers forever.

"What the hell happened?" he demanded, his voice still edged with his panic.

Tessie smiled. "Her VW Microbus broke down on Chestnut Street. She had to run the last six blocks on foot."

Finn began to chuckle again, and this time Sean couldn't help but join him. Oh, god. He just wanted to get this over with so he and Autumn could be alone together, embarking on the rest of their lives.

Tessie ducked back out then, and Sean's brothers filed out after her, the organ music swelling in volume as the five Monahan boys entered the sanctuary. Once they were situated, the organist segued into Pachelbel's Canon, and Sean turned to watch the bridesmaids' entry, each one looking elegant and beautiful and happy. And then the music changed again, to "The Wedding March" this time, and he stopped seeing anything at all. Because everything in the church—in the entire world—faded to nothing once he beheld Autumn Pulaski.

He'd seen her dressed in white scores of times—every time he'd stopped by the bakery. Every time he asked her to wear that white nightgown that was so arousing. But never had he seen her looking more beautiful than she did in that one transcendent moment. Her cheeks were pink from her recent exertion—or, perhaps, because of something else—and a few errant auburn curls had escaped her elaborately braided hairstyle. A thick crown of fresh white flowers encircled her head, and a gown of delicate white lace hugged her body with much affection. She carried a massive white bouquet of gardenias, and Sean didn't think he would ever get tired of looking at her.

Slowly, she made her way up the aisle, to Sean, to their life together. And the moment she was close enough for him to do it, he took her hand in his.

"I didn't think you were going to make it," he told her softly.

She grinned mischievously. "Are you kidding? After all the trouble I went to to get my hair like this?"

He fixed his gaze on hers, loving what he saw in the amber depths of her eyes. No, he would never get tired of looking at her. "I love you, Autumn," he said quietly. "Never leave me."

She smiled back. "I love you, Sean. And I never will."

They turned as one to face the priest, full of love, full of joy, full of happily ever after. Because both of them knew what challenges lay ahead, and both understood that they would never have to risk anything again.

*　*　*　*　*

January 2001
TALL, DARK & WESTERN
#1339 by Anne Marie Winston

February 2001
THE WAY TO A RANCHER'S HEART
#1345 by Peggy Moreland

March 2001
MILLIONAIRE HUSBAND
#1352 by Leanne Banks
Million-Dollar Men

April 2001
GABRIEL'S GIFT
#1357 by Cait London
Freedom Valley

May 2001
THE TEMPTATION OF
RORY MONAHAN
#1363 by Elizabeth Bevarly

June 2001
A LADY FOR LINCOLN CADE
#1369 by BJ James
Men of Belle Terre

MAN OF THE MONTH

For twenty years Silhouette has been giving
you the ultimate in romantic reads. Come join
the celebration as some of your favorite authors
help celebrate our anniversary with the most
sensual, emotional love stories ever!

Available at your favorite retail outlet.

Where love comes alive™

Visit Silhouette at www.eHarlequin.com   SDMOM01

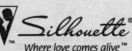

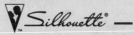

Silhouette®

where love comes alive—online...

eHARLEQUIN.com

your romantic books

♥ Shop online! Visit Shop eHarlequin and discover a wide selection of new releases and classic favorites at great discounted prices.

♥ Read our daily and weekly Internet exclusive serials, and participate in our interactive novel in the reading room.

♥ Ever dreamed of being a writer? Enter your chapter for a chance to become a featured author in our Writing Round Robin novel.

• • • • • • •

your romantic life

♥ Check out our feature articles on dating, flirting and other important romance topics and get your daily love dose with tips on how to keep the romance alive every day.

• • • • • • •

your community

♥ Have a Heart-to-Heart with other members about the latest books and meet your favorite authors.

♥ Discuss your romantic dilemma in the Tales from the Heart message board.

your romantic escapes

♥ Learn what the stars have in store for you with our daily Passionscopes and weekly Erotiscopes.

♥ Get the latest scoop on your favorite royals in Royal Romance.

COMING NEXT MONTH

CMN1200